# THE SUN KISSED SCROLLS

# Bright Paw

## RUBY ELLIS

"In each of us lie good and bad, light and dark, art and pain, choice and regret, cruelty and sacrifice. We're each of us our own chiaroscuro, our own bit of illusion fighting to emerge into something solid, something real."

—Libba Bray

# Content Warning

This book contains strong language, sexually explicit scenes, violence, death of a loved one (off page), kidnapping, and injury.
Bright Paw is intended for readers 18+.

# Pronunciation Guide

Mo Sholas: (mo hulas) is a Scottish Gaelic phrase translating to "my light" or "my solace" and is a term of endearment to describe someone who brings brightness, joy, or comfort to the speaker's life.

Mo Chridhe: (mo kree-uh) is a Scottish Gaelic phrase translating literally to "my heart" and is widely used as a term of endearment.

# Table of Contents

# 1

## The Invisible Life of Freya Banks

Freya

I used to think 'invisible' was just a metaphor. A dramatic word I used in the margins of my journals when I wanted to feel poetic. But now, floating somewhere between heartbeat and nothingness, I realize invisibility is real. Not just a trick of the light. But a place. A condition. My eternal actuality.

The machines beside me hum and beep in rhythm, mechanical breaths that fill the silence between the doctor's words. He speaks softly, like people do when they think the dying might hear them. My mother sniffles. My father clears his throat.

"She's stable for now," the doctor says. "But the brain activity hasn't changed much since she arrived."

Well, that can't be good.

There's a pause thick enough to drown in. It isn't the first time that my lack of response has harshed the vibe.

"How much longer will we have to stay here?" My father asks. "I have a meeting tomorrow."

Of course he does. Even now, with tubes in my throat and a needle in my arm, he's thinking about quarterly reports and investors. I wish I could roll my eyes, maybe cough just to make him look at me. But my body is a locked door and I don't have the key.

My mother's voice is tight, shaking in that way she gets before she starts to cry or drink—sometimes both. "What am I supposed to tell people?" she asks.

I can just picture the doctor's face—thinking that he was having a difficult conversation with my grieving, loving parents. But instead, he is forced to answer insensitive questions like *what is the socially acceptable amount of time to wait before pulling the plug?* And, *what will our friends at the club think about our daughter getting hit by a car because she was out until bar close?*

All of their words are thick with judgment.

I want to scream.

Not that the truth matters to them, but I wasn't drinking. Sloane and I were waiting for our friend, Willa's, shift to end so that we could give her a ride home. We were supposed to laugh about Sloane's dating misadventures and Willa's stories of what people confess when they have had one too many pints of Guinness. But instead, tires screeched, glass shattered, and now, I'm here.

And they're not.

The doctor said as much.

Willa was killed on impact, having tried to shield us from the speeding car. Sloane was stuck in the car as it went up in flames. She made it to the hospital but succumbed to her injuries shortly after.

Me? I was found outside of the car, like something had pushed me—removed me. It probably would have been a miracle if I could have landed on anything other than my head. So now I am just here. Listening. Fading.

Willa and Sloane were my only constants in a world that pretended I was decoration. We met in a church basement when we were children. Three little kids with heart defects. We used to joke that we were invincible because our hearts were already broken—how could we not survive everything else?

That was until the crash proved that even patched up hearts can stop beating.

My father sighs, impatient. "She shouldn't have been out that late anyway. She needs to take responsibility for her actions."

I want to laugh. A dry, brittle laugh that doesn't need air to breathe.

Responsibility? Hah! As if he has ever taken responsibility for anything in his life.

The doctor murmurs something about hope and recovery. About how it's too early to give up. He reminds them that I am only 25 years old. That I could wake up.

My mother scoffs at his suggestion that I could live a normal life. Not because he is suggesting that I could come out of this okay but because she doesn't believe I could ever live up to their version of normal, even before the accident.

A mid-sized, independent woman who would rather hide away in my art studio than get my ass grabbed by whatever business partner my father has around? Scandal.

*Normal* has never been the standard that they set for me. Neither was *happy.*

I start to drift, still floating in the nothingness but falling further into the deep.

It's strange how being unseen feels familiar—comforting. It shouldn't, but my whole life has been a quiet rehearsal for this moment. Sitting at dinner while my parents performed their version of perfection. Ignoring the long line of mistresses and pills that they used to dull their own inadequacies. Smiling through it all, as if it could just be forgotten if it is ignored. Like me.

Even now, I'm the centerpiece of the room, the reason they're here, and yet I'm still invisible.

I want to move.

I want to open my eyes.

I want to trade their apathy for a few minutes of quiet.

But then something changes.

The machines fade into a soft hum. The voices into whispers. And there it is—a light. Bright to the point of blindness, but vital to everything that I am. It feels warm. Gentle. Forgiving.

There is no fear. No hesitation. Just a pull—like gravity in reverse.

For once, I don't think about what my parents will say or how the papers will phrase the accident. I don't think about being invisible or broken or unloved.

I think about Willa's laugh. I think about Sloane's stupid puns.

I think about how alive we felt just hours ago.

And then I walk forward.

Into the light.

Into something that finally—*finally*—sees me.

# 2

## The Keeper of the Keep

Casimir

The wind sighs through the crack in the old stones, carrying the faint scent of pine and the ghost of smoke that never quite left these walls. I sit behind my father's desk—what's left of it—running my thumb over the deep scars that blemish the surface.

He used to sit here, maps and ledgers before him, his laughter echoing off these very walls. Now, the laughter is just a memory. The warmth, the noise, the smell of roast and honey—all gone.

The keep is a tomb and I am its keeper.

Five years.

Five years since the night the rebels came.

They believe themselves to be liberators, champions of the 'new dawn.'

They believe that the old ways, the Sun Kissed, are relics of a dying age. That those of us who still carry the blessings within our lines are hoarders of our sacred gold and superstition.

And so, they came in the dark, torches high, claws sharpened, and fury stoked by envy.

I was away.

I had gone deep into the mountains to find a medicine for a fever that had taken hold of the cubs. If I had returned a few hours earlier, I would have burned along with my family.

My father.

My mother.

My sister Liora.

The smell of ash still finds me in my dreams.

The rebels took everything of value as the flames licked the stone walls of the keep. Gold. Weapons. But they didn't find it all. Deep beneath the keep, in chambers they never breached, lies what they sought most: the sacred Sun Kissed Scrolls.

The scrolls are more than parchment and ink. They hold the history of the Sun Kissed. The knowledge of the Firsts. The teachings of The Sun Goddess herself. And with it, they carry the light of prophecy—the promise that one day, the greed and blood lust that poisons this land will burn itself out, and the blessed will rise to restore the balance.

It's a fragile hope, but it's all that we have left.

I look up at the map pinned to the wall, its edges curled and fraying. It details the entire bear territory, crude lines drawn on to depict how it has been divided by the three remaining Sun Kissed clans.

It wasn't always this way. Clans had their keeps, of course, but the land itself remained whole, belonging to everyone. But with the rebels moving through, carving out space that shouldn't belong to any of us, we needed to find a way to monitor everything effectively.

My clan maintains peace in the northern portion of our land, through the mountains and into the deep cold of the ice forests.

The Claw clan is through the mountain pass, stretching south and meeting the border with the wolves and panthers.

Maw takes the rest, spanning to the sea.

It has been years since I have seen my friends, communicating through carrier birds while we keep our locations protected. It isn't ideal, but it is the best we can do.

My clan, having been decimated to near extinction, now consists of myself and nine others. Four are my cousins. The rest are old family friends. Ten of us protecting a third of the territory from those who want us erased.

The door creaks open.

I know the footsteps before I see him—soft but weighted, the quiet tread of someone who's learned to move unseen. Kiran, my cousin, steps in, the wind following him like a ghost. His face is hard, his eyes colder than the mountain air.

"They're coming," he says without preamble.

I straighten in my chair. "How many?"

"Too many for comfort. A dozen. Maybe more. They are moving through the lower pass," Kiran continues. "They'll reach the valley by tomorrow if they keep pace."

I push back from the desk, the chair's legs scraping across the stone floor. "They can't reach the valley. If they do, they'll find the entrances to the lower caverns."

He nods grimly. "I know."

For a long moment, we stand in silence, the fire crackling low between us. The thought of leaving this place— the one bit of safety we've managed to reclaim—gnaws at me. We have little food. Fewer weapons. And no reinforcements. But if the rebels find the tunnels...

"They'll take everything," I say quietly. "And this time, they won't leave without the gold and The Scrolls."

Kiran's gaze meets mine. "Then we fight."

I draw a slow breath, the weight of the years pressing down on my chest. "We'll take the mountain pass. Push them back before they set foot in the valley."

He gives a short nod. "We'll need everyone."

"Some will need to stay behind to protect the keep," I say, bitterness curling through the words. "We might need them in the fight, but we can't risk leaving it unguarded."

I walk to the window slit, looking out at the frozen peaks bathed in the pale light of dawn. Somewhere beyond those ridges lies the rest of the world—thriving, scheming, forgetting us. Let them. The Paw will rise again.

"The prophecy," I murmur, half to myself. "It talks of a sister's might and rising from the shadows and back into the light."

Kiran huffs. "And you think that is us?"

I let a faint smile tug at my lips. "I think that we are the ones who keep that light from going out."

He doesn't argue. He knows better.

I turn back to him, resolve settling into my bones like stone. "Ready the others. We move before dusk."

"As you will, Chief."

When he leaves, I linger a moment longer, listening to the wind moan through the empty halls. I reach beneath the desk, to the hidden compartment my father built long before I was born. My fingers find the small brass latch. It clicks open, revealing the gleam of gold beneath.

Not much. There are piles hidden safely under the keep. But this will be enough to tempt any rebel dog who catches its scent.

I close it gently, whispering an old blessing under my breath.

"By the light that kissed the dawn, guard what remains."

Then I rise. The time for hiding is done. If the prophecy is to live, it will be written in blood and fire—ours or theirs.

# 3

## A Spark

Casimir

The mountain pass is a narrow, jagged scar between two ancient peaks. Snow drifts through the air, glittering like shards of broken light, and the wind cuts through fur and flesh alike. It doesn't matter that it is the warmer season—up here in the mountains, winter never fully recedes.

We move in silence. Six shadows stalking in the light.

We have fought before, but never quite like this. Not with our backs pressed against the edge of extinction. The scent of them reaches me first—rebels. Bear-born, just like us, but tainted by greed and hunger for power. The stench of sweat, blood, and too many bodies living in close proximity.

Bears are not pack animals like the wolves. We prefer space, small families, and clans that span enough distance to let us breathe. Or that is how it was before the rebels attacked, forcing a change.

I raise my hand, signaling the others to hold. We traveled most of the way in fur but shifted into our smaller forms once we got close, allowing us to remain undetected.

"Half a dozen ahead," Kiran says quietly as he crouches next to me. "More beyond, near the ridge."

I nod. "We strike fast. Loud. We drive them back before they know what hit them."

He grins—a flash of teeth. "Just how you like it."

He's not wrong. The pull inside me, that old, violent rhythm, has been rising since we left the keep. The longer I ignore it, the harder it claws at me. It's more than instinct. More than fury. It feels like something is calling me forward, a tug deep in my chest, humming beneath my ribs.

I have always felt a stronger pull of magic out in these wooded trees, as if The Mother is always there. Watching. Protecting.

But this feels different.

Deciding that it is time to strike, I let the shift rip through me like lightning—bones grinding, muscles stretching, fur bursting through my skin. Despite the gruesome appearance of the shift, it is a smooth, painless transition.

My roar rattles the trees around us, signaling our attack now that we are upon them. Blurry-eyed, still trying to sleep off their ale from the night before, the rebels don't stand a chance.

We hit them like an avalanche, overwhelming them before they had a chance to organize. Claws flash, fangs rend, and the ground stains red. I tear through two before they can even shift, their screams scattering into the wind. One manages to take bear form—a hulking brute who must be this clan's leader based on the rebel mark branded on his chest. I crush him beneath my weight, my jaws finding his throat.

The fight is chaos and fury and memory all tangled together. For a heartbeat, I see my sister's face, hear her laughter before it turns into screams.

Rage fuels me.

Retribution fuels me.

My power, my purpose fuels me.

Every blow that I land is struck with my responsibility to my bloodline. The Sun Kissed blessing that runs through my veins, the ancient magic that I feel swirling in the wind of the forest, encourages me to continue.

If my mother and sister were here, they would use their power to send lashes of sunlight burning through our enemies.

But they are gone.

So, I will fight in their honor.

It is over within minutes. The bears that Kiran had scouted further away vanished during the fight. Those that stayed have no chance of walking out of here. Bears may be difficult to kill, but we know not to leave any survivors.

I look to my clan, panting now that the fight has ceased. Their steaming breath rises before them like ghosts.

We've won—but something is wrong.

The pull in my chest hasn't faded. It's stronger. Urgent.

"Caz?" Kiran asks, his voice rough, wary. "What is it?"

"I don't know," I tell him, rubbing my chest. "But something's—"

Then I hear it.

A heartbeat. Faint, fragile. And calling to mine.

I turn towards the sound. Toward the cliffs just on the other side of the rebel's camp. Toward what feels like the very core of my soul.

The others follow as I climb over large boulders, scaling a small ledge of the cliff, before arriving at a cave filled with supplies. Furs. Tools. Stolen gold. And a female.

She is small—much smaller than bear shifter females. Her breaths wheeze out of her in pained gasps. She is filthy. Bruised. Her scraps of clothing are in tatters. Her wrists are bound with rope behind her back and her skin is broken, clawed up all over her body.

An acute pain stutters through my chest, so sharp I drop to my knees before her, unable to keep standing.

Her scent thickens in the air, cherry and almond becoming sweeter in my company. But bitterness remains as well, tickling my senses. Fear. And something older. A scent that hits me hard in the chest.

The pain recedes moments before my heart stops. For a long, shuddering moment, I think that I have died. Simply ceased to exist in her presence. Then—*thump*. It starts again, harder, faster...but it's not my rhythm anymore. It is hers. Ours. Our hearts beat together, marvelously matched as if she is alive within my chest. A perfect echo.

Heart Mates.

A bond I have long given up on ever finding.

A tie stronger, more sacred than life itself.

I inch closer, my fingers trembling as I use a shifted claw to cut through the ropes binding her wrists.

"Easy," I murmur, my voice low, my bear rumbling beneath my words. "You are safe now."

But she flinches from me, scrambling back, eyes wide with terror.

"Don't—please—don't hurt me," she whispers in a foreign tongue. Her voice is hoarse, her lips cracked.

"You are not one of them," I say softly, switching to her language. It is not a question. Looking closer at her clothing, it is clear that she is not from this territory.

She shakes her head weakly. "They found me. Took me." She takes a few more pained breaths, looking into my eyes, her own softening. "I don't understand. They saw this, but I don't understand." She moves the fabric away from her chest, flashing me a small portion of the delicate skin on her breasts—just enough for me to recognize the Sun Kissed mark that glitters on her pale skin.

She is not from here, yet she is Sun Kissed? I do not understand how this is possible.

Kiran approaches slowly, maintaining enough distance from this female so that she does not feel threatened. "Who is she?"

"I don't know." But the truth thrums through me, deep and undeniable. "She is *mine.*"

The female looks up at me, confusion and fear warring in her eyes. But underneath it, there is an unmistakable, innate trust.

I reach out, letting my hand hover near hers. "You are safe," I say again, this time pouring the weight of every vow, every loss, every heartbeat into my words. "By the light that kissed the dawn," I whisper, "no one will hurt you again."

The prophecy spoke of a Sister's Might, rising from the dark and burning the greed from the land.

I think I've just found a spark.

# 4

## *I'd Like to Speak with the Manager*

Freya

The light was supposed to mean peace.

Or heaven. Or, honestly, I would have settled for a good long nap.

But instead of angels or harps or some overly polite St. Peter with a clipboard, I wake up face first in snow.

Cold. Bitterly cold. It burns my lungs when I breathe and stings my fingers when I move. Snowflakes cling to my eyelashes, and when I sit up, a wave of dizziness nearly knocks me flat again. For a moment, all I can do is stare at the trees. Frozen branches standing tall among the mountains that surround us. Everything is silent except the wind sighing through the ice forest.

I blink a few times, trying to remember. Was it all a dream?

The car. The crash. The blinding light.

I was sure that it was—that I crossed over. I left my parents in that hospital room as they discussed how inconvenient it was of me to be in a coma.

"Okay," I mutter, hugging my arms around myself. "If this is heaven, someone needs to talk to management. I was expecting clouds and maybe a buffet."

My stomach growled in agreement. Loudly.

"Right, food. Do ghosts even get hungry?" I frowned down at myself. I am definitely not dressed for the weather. The hospital gown and robe are all that I have on. My shoes are gone. My skin is icy, but I can still *feel* everything. So...not a ghost. Or maybe ghosts just had better pain receptors than I'd been led to believe.

I get to my feet, wobbling. The snow is ankle-deep, and every step makes my toes ache. The forest stretches endlessly in every direction—no road, no sign of people, just frost and silence.

"Okay, Freya," I tell myself, because talking to myself is better than freezing to death quietly. "If the pearly gates are out here, they're probably past the next pine tree."

Or maybe the next.

Or the next.

I don't know how long I walk. Long enough for my lips to split and my fingers to go numb. Long enough that the sky turns dusky and my legs start to tremble. Just when I am about to give up and lie down—because honestly, I can't think of anything that sounds better at the moment, I see it.

A flicker of orange.

Smoke.

I stumble toward it, heart thudding. The small clearing ahead holds a ring of stones, a few logs, and the faint warmth of dying embers. Someone had been here—recently. I sink beside the pit and hold my hands over it, desperate for the little heat it still offers.

"Thank you, mystery camper," I whisper, closing my eyes. "I owe you one heavenly latte."

But the camp is empty. A few footprints, a torn scrap of cloth, and no food. My stomach twisted again, reminding me that hunger in the afterlife was apparently a thing. I stay by the fire as long as I dare before exhaustion drags me under.

The days blur after that. I follow the trail—bits of disturbed snow, footprints leading deeper into the mountains. Each night, I find another camp, another fading fire, and no people. It becomes my only goal: find them. Whoever *they* are. They had food. They had warmth. They had answers.

By the fourth day, I was half delirious with hunger. My legs shake with every step, and the cold sinks deep into my bones. When I finally see movement ahead—figures, dark and human-shaped—relief floods through me so hard I nearly cry.

"Hey!" My voice cracks. "Please! Wait—help!"

They turn. Eight men, huge and broad-shouldered, wearing furs and leather. Their eyes glint amber in the dim light. For a heartbeat, I think I am saved.

Then their shapes began to ripple.

Bones crack. Skin stretches.

And where men had stood, there were now *bears*. Enormous, snarling, angry-eyed bears.

I freeze, too shocked even to scream. One of them growls, a deep, rumbling sound that vibrates through my chest. Then they stop—staring not at my face, but at my chest.

I look down. The faint light caught on something—an intricate, golden mark shaped like a sunburst, glimmering on my breast.

"I—I don't—" was all I managed before the world tilted and went black.

When I wake, my hands are tied behind me, wrists raw from the rope. My head pounds. The shifters—men again now—are talking, laughing cruelly. Every word is rough, mocking. I can't understand what they are saying, but their tone tells me enough. They push me when I stumble, yanking me along the trail like a broken doll.

By the time we stop for the night, I can barely walk. Cuts and bruises color my skin as they fester despite the freezing weather. They shove me into a cave stocked with furs, crates, and weapons. My breath comes in small, shaky clouds. I should have been grateful for the walls, the brief warmth. Instead, I feel the cold twist of dread in my gut.

I am not going to make it out of here alive.

Then came the shouting.

Outside—the clash of claws, the roar of battle. My captors scream, snarl, then go silent. I curl myself into a tighter ball, heart hammering, as I pray for this nightmare to end.

Footsteps.

From the corner of my eye, I watch as a figure ducks inside. Another giant of a man, easily seven feet tall, his skin dark as obsidian, his short hair gleaming with golden rings that catch the firelight. His eyes—impossibly—were violet. His naked body is corded with muscles. He is powerful. But he approaches gently.

He kneels beside me and says something low, in a language that must be the same as what my captors spoke, but unlike the harsh tone that they used, from him, it sounds beautiful. I don't respond, unsure as to how to communicate with him.

He grabs at his chest; pain is clear in his eyes. But he does not move away. He stays next to me as if he cannot bring himself to leave my side.

A beat later, pain flares in mine. My heart stutters—then stops.

I gasp, panic clawing up my throat—then it *starts again*, thudding in a new rhythm that isn't quite mine.

"Don't—please—don't hurt me," I whispered, trembling.

He looks at me then, really looks, and the fear drains away like water from a cracked cup. There is something in his gaze—something that feels like safety, like warmth after endless cold.

Slowly, I tug at the torn scraps of my clothes and show him the sunburst mark.

"They found me," I say, wanting to explain. "I don't understand. They saw this, but I don't understand."

He reaches out, tracing the mark with a hand so gentle it makes my throat ache. His eyes soften. When he speaks again, his voice was a promise.

"You are safe," he says—this time, in words I somehow understand. "No one will hurt you again."

And I believe him.

As the world dims at the edges, I let myself fall into his arms, into the strange heartbeat that isn't quite mine.

Then everything goes dark.

# 5

## Heart Mates

Casimir

The smell of blood and fear still clings to the cave walls. It mixes with her scent—sweet cherries and crushed almonds. Fainter now, soured by exhaustion and pain. My Heart Mate lies motionless in my arms, her breaths too shallow, her skin too pale.

I brush a strand of tangled hair from her face, my chest tightening. "If we hadn't found her tonight…"

Kiran crouches beside me, his eyes narrowing as he studies her. "She's not one of ours, Caz. No bear blood runs in her veins. Look, she's too small. Too fragile."

I glance down at her breast where the sacred Sun Kissed mark shimmers gold beneath the grime and tattered fabric, pulsing in time with her slowing heartbeat. It is impossible. Only the blessed lines carry such a mark— chosen by The Sun Goddess herself. Passed down through the lines, the blessed females carry the mark. But they were all killed by the rebels. My mother, my sister—every grandmother, mother, sister—murdered by the greed of the rebel clans. How is it possible for a non-bear to carry such a mark?

"I know," I agree quietly. "But the bond sang to me the moment I saw her. She is my Heart Mate. Our Heart Strings are tied together as one."

Kiran shakes his head in disbelief. "Then what is she? She smells...different. Feels different. And this—" he gestures to her torn clothing—"is not from our world."

Before I can answer, our cousin Bran strides closer. "I have heard rumors from the wolf lands," he says. "They say strange females fell from the sky—witches, some called them. Claimed they stole magic, warped it. But then..." His gaze flicks to the unconscious woman in my arms. "Those same witches turned out to be the Alphas' True Mates. Moon Touched, all three of them. Marked like her."

"Moon Touched?" Kiran echoes softly, frowning. "And she's Sun Kissed. But how? Why?"

Bran shrugs.

Regardless of what her being Sun Kissed might mean for us, the only truth that matters right now is that she needs help. "We can't stay here." I shift her carefully against my chest. "She needs warmth. Food. Safety."

Kiran nods his agreement. "Ride on my back. I'll carry you both."

I hesitate. Riding another bear is not our way—too intimate, too submissive a gesture—but Kiran meets my eyes with steady resolve. "You're our Chief, Caz. Let me help you."

I incline my head. "Thank you, cousin."

Moments later, I am astride his broad back, my Mate wrapped in furs against me. Her head rests beneath my chin, and I can feel the faint flutter of her pulse. "Hold on," I whisper, though she cannot hear me. "Please. Hold on."

We race through the frozen forest, the ground breaking beneath Kiran's paws, moonlight spilling silver over the trees. On the other side of the mountain pass, the air would be warm. But here, the wind bites my skin as I shield my Mate from its chill. I press her closer. By the time the keep's gates come into view, sitting like ribs of an ancient beast against the mountainside, her pulse is a mere flutter.

Inside, I lay her on my bed—our bed, though she doesn't know it yet. I heat water, scrub the dirt and blood from her body, each bruise another knife in my chest. Her ribs are broken. Claw marks rake her sides. I can smell infection setting in—sickly, sour, a death scent no shifter should ever carry due to our accelerated healing.

She should be healing.

Why isn't she healing?

Hours pass. Her breathing grows weaker. Her heartbeat—our heartbeat—falters.

"The bond," I whisper, realization slamming through me. "It's the only way."

Kiran stiffens by the doorway. "Caz, if you bind yourself to her now, and she dies—"

"Then I might die with her." I meet his gaze without flinching. "I know that."

"She's not strong enough," he argues. "You don't even know if she *wants* this."

"I know," I rasp. "But if I do nothing, she'll be gone before we ever had an opportunity to know each other. The bonding sun rises tomorrow. It's our only chance."

Kiran runs a hand through his hair, cursing softly. "You're mad, cousin. Completely mad."

"Maybe," I say. "But I'd rather die trying to save her than live knowing I didn't."

He doesn't try to stop me after that.

When dawn's first light spills into the sky, I carry her into the garden behind the keep. Frost gleams on the stone. The air hums with the rising magic of the bonding sun, that rare and sacred moment when The Sun Goddess blesses all unions of soul and heart.

I kneel with her in my arms. Her face is serene now, her lips parted as if she dreams of something gentler than this world.

"I'm sorry," I whisper. "I wish you could choose this with me. I wish we had time. But I can't lose you."

I bend my head, pressing my lips to her hair. "If you wake, and do not want me, I'll step aside. I'll protect you still, from a distance if I must. But live. Please, live."

The sun crests the horizon, flooding the world in pink and gold. Power ripples through me, ancient and wild. My bear roars inside my chest, claiming, binding, needing.

I sink my teeth into the soft curve of her neck.

Our magic explodes between us—blinding, searing and pure.

Her scream rips through the morning air, and her body arches in my arms. For a heartbeat, I fear I've killed her. Then her hands clutch at me, fingers digging into my shoulders, and her eyes snap open—bright with the fire of the sun.

She's alive.

She gasps, and the sound shatters me. But I cannot stop now that it has started. A bond left half completed is a death sentence.

Wrapping my hand around the back of her neck, I firmly guide her mouth to my skin, pressing just enough to break the flesh with her teeth.

I can feel it—as soon as she gives in. Her back bows in my arms, the sunrise brightening and casting us in a warm glow. My Mate bites down harder, moaning as my blood fills her mouth.

Our bond snaps into place like a string going taut, threading between us like molten gold. Searing. Fusing. Belonging.

Her heartbeat slams into rhythm once more with mine. For a moment, the magic collides so violently that I can't breathe. Then, it evens out, syncing steady and strong.

Her life rushes back into her body. I can *feel* it.

She collapses against me once more, trembling, her breath ragged. I cradle her close, whispering against her temple, "Easy. You're safe now. You're safe."

Her scent—cherries, almonds, and now sunlight—fills the garden. The infection's sour rot is gone, burned away by the bond's cleansing fire. The bruises fade before my eyes, claw marks knitting shut. Even the deep cuts along her ribs close, leaving only faint silver traces.

It worked. Sun Goddess, it worked.

I exhale a shaky breath of relief and pull her closer, one arm around her waist, the other stroking her hair. Her skin is hot beneath my fingers, too hot, but alive. So alive.

Then she moves. Slowly, her hands push against my chest. I loosen my hold, giving her space.

She blinks up at me, pupils wide, irises a shade I've never seen—brown, like bark but highlighted with shimmering gold. She speaks, her voice hoarse and foreign. I don't recognize the words, but the magic of my kind twists them into meaning.

"Where am I?"

I swallow hard. "You're safe," I tell her softly. "You're home."

She frowns, gaze darting past me to the frost-dusted stones of the courtyard, the tall walls of the keep rising around us. Her brow creases deeper. "This isn't possible."

Her accent is strange—sharp and smooth all at once, carrying the lilt of a world untouched by our wild lands.

"You were dying," I say, my voice low. "You'd been hurt—starved. The rebels..." My jaw tightens. "They nearly broke you."

Her eyes darken, memories flashing through them. She flinches, curling inward, and instinct drives me closer. I cup her cheek, forcing gentleness into my touch. "They can't hurt you again. I swear it."

She looks at me then—really looks. "Who are you?"

I almost laugh, but the sound catches in my throat. "Casimir," I say. "Caz. Chief of the Paw Clan. And you..." I hesitate, because the truth feels like something too heavy to place on her fragile shoulders. "...you are my Heart Mate."

She stills. Confusion crosses her face, followed by disbelief. "Your what?"

"The one chosen by fate. By The Sun Goddess herself. My heart's other half."

Her lips part, but no sound comes. She stares at me as though I've spoken madness. And maybe I have—to her, a stranger who has fallen between worlds.

Her fingers rise to her neck where my teeth had pierced her skin. The wound has healed to a faint crescent of gold. She touches it, eyes wide, voice trembling. "You bit me."

"Yes," I admit quietly. "To bond us. It was the only way to save your life."

Her pulse leaps under my fingertips and in my heart, fast and erratic. "You *bonded* me?"

"I didn't have a choice," I say, the words rough, desperate. "You were dying. I couldn't—" I break off, shaking my head. "I couldn't lose you."

Silence falls. The dawn wind curls around us, carrying the scent of pine and frost.

Finally, she whispers, "You don't even know me."

"I know enough," I answer, and the truth burns in my chest. "I know that when I found you, my heart stopped until you breathed again. I know the Sun Kissed mark on your skin means that you are meant to be in this world. And I know that the bond would not have been answered if you were not meant for me."

Her throat works as she swallows. "Meant for you..."

She looks away, tears gathering in her lashes. "Back home, no one would ever say something like that. Not about *me.*"

My fingers tilt her chin back toward me. "Then your home was blind."

For a long time, neither of us speak. The light of the bonding sun fades to soft morning gold. The world seems to hold its breath around us.

Kiran's voice breaks the silence from the edge of the garden. "She's awake, then."

I nod, not taking my eyes off her. "She's alive."

The woman—my Mate—stares at me, confusion and something like fear in her gaze.

"I don't know what any of this means," she whispers. "I don't know where I am. Or what I am."

I take her hand, gently, reverently. "Then I'll help you find out," I promise. "You're not alone anymore."

And though I mean every word, a cold knot twists deep in my chest—because I can still feel the echo of her fear through the bond.

She doesn't trust me. She doesn't accept me.

And I don't know what to do about that.

# 6

## Bears, Beets, Battlestar Galactica

Freya

How many times do I need to experience death before it actually sticks?

First there was the bright light—the one that I thought would bring me to the afterlife, but instead brought me here, to this other world where people turn into animals in the blink of an eye.

Then, there was the dark. The deepest dark that I fell into before a blinding, searing light washed over me and left me with a bite mark on my neck and more questions than could possibly be answered in a lifetime.

There are parts of this world that feel like they might be heaven, like the very large man who is watching me like I'm a particularly fragile bomb about to go off.

My mouth is dry, my head is pounding, and my body—well, it doesn't hurt. It *should* hurt. Last I remember, I was knocking on death's door. Again.

The man—mountain, really—leans forward, his corded muscles tensing with the movement. His voice a low rumble as he reassures me that I am safe.

"Are you sure this isn't the afterlife?" I ask, needing to double check. Because people were not this beautiful in real life.

His lips twitch. "You are not dead."

"Damn. Just one more thing to add to my list of failures," I joke.

He makes a sound that's half amusement, half concern, and for some reason, that makes my chest ache. I shouldn't feel comforted by someone I don't know, but the moment my eyes met his—a vibrant, impossible violet—I felt safe. Like my nervous system got the memo before my brain did.

He introduced himself as Casimir. Caz. Offering me the use of his nickname as if we know each other well enough for that.

As I stare at him, he explains again that he is a bear shifter. That he doesn't believe I am from this world. And that we are bonded with a blessing of sacred, ancient magic.

Right. Sure. And I'm the Tooth Fairy. What does it even mean? How can it be possible? I mean, I know that I saw my captors change from man to bear, but I was half hoping that it was some weird psychedelic dream. That I accidentally ingested a funky fungus and was blitzed out of my mind.

Except, when he says the word *bonded*, I feel a pulse in my chest that doesn't belong to me. Two beats, then one, syncing together. Mine and his. As if my heart restarted for him alone.

He explains more, patient but uncertain. He says that he had to bond with me to save my life. That there is magic in this world. And that we are Heart Mates, which sounds like another name for soulmates. Casimir does not know what it'll mean for me since I am not a shifter—apparently, he can tell from my scent, which doesn't make me self-conscious at all—but he *thinks* that with accelerated healing, it might also help me to live a longer life. I guess shifters can live for over 1000 years.

Great. I'm a medical mystery *and* magically hitched to a bear.

I ask for time alone, because my brain feels like it's been shoved into a blender. He hesitates but agrees, leading me into a bedroom before leaving me with an apology in his eyes and a view of back muscles that shouldn't be legal.

When he's gone, I try to make sense of things.

Magic.

Bonded.

Bears.

Beets.

Battlestar Galactica.

I sigh. What I wouldn't give to let a restorative binge of The Office work its magic on my brain right now.

There are other shifters in this world too. Other bears, like my captors with their cruel laughter and rough hands. They spoke words that I didn't understand. But now, somehow, I understand *him*. The language slips effortlessly into my mind, and he says it's because of the bond.

Wonderful. A magical translation feature. Just what every coma patient turned world-hopping kidnapping victim needs.

When Casimir comes back, he's carrying a tray of food that smells heavenly. My stomach growls loud enough to embarrass me, but I dig in anyway. Manners can wait until after calories. He asks for my name, and I realize I never told him.

"Freya," I say through a mouthful of bread. "Sorry. Dying kind of distracted me from introductions."

His mouth tilts in something like a smile before he leaves again, giving me space.

Later, I make my way into the bathroom and wash up. The water is cold, but it wakes me up, grounds me. My reflection looks...different. Healthier. My skin glows faintly, and my bruises are gone. I remember the pain—the broken ribs, the cuts, the infection—but my body's whole now.

Back in bed, I fall asleep quickly, but my dreams are cruel reminders of what I went through. Chicago. My studio apartment that I was so proud to pay for on my own, not even allowing my trust fund to help. Something that was completely mine, not handed to me in an effort to make my parents seem generous to their friends. Paint-stained hands as I worked on my commissioned pieces. Willa's laughter. Sloane's terrible attempts at making coffee. And then—glass shattering, metal screeching. The crash.

I wake up gasping, heart hammering.

Casimir is there instantly, like he'd been waiting. He grips my hand, his big thumb brushing over my knuckles. His flawless, dark skin is in beautiful contrast with my own. His voice is gentle. "You're safe," he reminds me.

And I *believe* him. That's the worst part.

But then I remember what he said—he bonded with me because he *had* to. Not because he wanted to. And the thought hits me like a stone to the chest.

I pull my hand away, curling up in the corner of the bed, knees to my chest. "You don't have to do that," I whisper.

He looks stricken. "I can feel your distress," he says, touching his chest. "It's part of the bond. Our hearts are connected. One beat."

I *can* feel it. His calm pushing against my panic. I just can't admit it.

He apologizes softly, like he's the one who's done something wrong, and says he'll give me space. When he leaves, he glances back once. It shouldn't matter. But it does.

I lie back down, pretending to sleep.

But my mind won't stop.

Willa and Sloane are gone. Am I dead too? Back in Chicago? Part of me wonders if that's easier for everyone, for my parents. I was never enough for them anyway—not successful enough, not obedient enough, not normal enough.

Now I'm magically bonded to a man who turns into a bear and probably regrets ever meeting me.

Still, I can't ignore how I feel when he's near. The warmth. The safety. The inexplicable rightness.

Maybe it's just the bond talking. Maybe it's real. Either way, I need answers.

As the early light of dawn creeps through the curtains, I make a silent promise to myself.

If I'm stuck in this world, I'm going to understand it. Every rule. Every secret. Every reason why a bear shifter with a haunted gaze and hands too gentle for his size would risk everything to save *me*.

And maybe—just maybe—why part of me already feels like he is my home.

I drift off but morning refuses to let me stay asleep.

Apparently, near-death experiences don't come with the courtesy of sleeping in. Sunlight slices through the curtains like it has a personal vendetta against my eyes. My head feels stuffed with fog and half-remembered dreams—paint, laughter, fire, a pair of purple eyes.

Right. The bear man. The magical bond. The not-dead part.

I groan and flop onto my stomach, burying my face in the pillow. It smells faintly like cedar and smoke and something warm I don't have a name for. Probably him. I tell myself I don't notice, but my traitor brain files the scent away under *comforting things I should not find comforting*.

My stomach growls. Loudly. I guess magic bonding doesn't come with complimentary breakfast refills.

I sit up slowly, testing my limbs. Still no pain. Still weird. I'm half expecting a crack or twinge, but I feel fine. Better than fine. Stronger, even.

The castle is quiet except for the steady crackle of the fire. Casimir isn't in the chair where he was before. The room feels bigger without him in it, and for some reason, that annoys me.

I spot my reflection again in the mirror near the bathroom door and pause. The faint glow I noticed last night is still there, like there's light just beneath my skin. Not bright enough to be alarming—just there, lighting up my chest.

"So that's new," I mutter. "Are human night lights a normal thing here?"

The mirror, unhelpfully, doesn't answer. I guess this isn't an enchanted castle.

I find a soft shirt draped over the chair—definitely not mine, definitely his—and slip it on anyway. It hangs past my thighs and smells like him. I look ridiculous and feel weirdly safe. Again, brain, *stop that.*

I step out into the hall. The place is cozy. Cabin-core Pinterest would weep with joy. Wood beams, shelves filled with books, furs scattered across the stone floors. Outside the windows, I glimpse trees stretching forever—ancient and shadowed, like the forest itself is watching.

I'm about to go exploring when the door opens, and Casimir steps inside.

If I thought he looked big before, seeing him in daylight ruins any sense of proportion I had left. He's massive. Broad shoulders, rich skin pulled tight across his bare chest, hair still damp from—what, a river bath? An early morning run?

He freezes when he sees me in his shirt, the one that he clearly forgot to put on this morning. His eyes darken slightly, then he looks away, clearing his throat. "You're up."

"Observant," I deadpan.

His mouth twitches. "I didn't want to wake you. You needed rest."

"Yeah, well, the sun didn't get that memo."

He leads me into a dining room where a table is piled with food—eggs, bread, something that smells suspiciously like bacon. "Eat," he says simply.

I sit, and for a while, the only sounds are utensils and me trying not to stare. When I finish, I look up at him. "So. You said yesterday you don't know much about what happens when a human gets bonded to a shifter."

He nods slowly. "It's never been recorded, as far as I know. My cousin told me that the wolves' human mates gain longevity, healing, and a bit of their partner's magic. But it's just a rumor. I do not know if it is true."

"And you just—did it?"

His gaze meets mine, steady. "You were dying. I reacted. I just—felt the bond reach for me."

Something flutters painfully behind my ribs. I hate that part of me wants to believe there was more to it than survival instinct. "So, it wasn't exactly a choice."

He flinches. "If I hadn't, you'd be gone."

"Right," I say, stabbing at my bread. "So, I'm basically a magical charity case."

His jaw tightens, but his voice stays soft. "You're alive. That's what matters."

It should sound comforting, but instead it lands heavy. Because he's right—it *is* what matters. But I can't stop wondering what comes next.

He stands, noticing that I have finished eating, and begins clearing our plates from the table. "If you feel well enough, I can show you around the keep. It might help you understand where you are. You can meet others in the clan."

"Keep," I repeat. "As in—this castle? Are there others who live here as well?"

"Some." He leads me back out through the door we entered through. "Our clan is not as large as it once was, but everyone who remains here at the keep will protect you."

Protect me? "Am I in danger?" I ask. "The men who captured me. Will they come after me?"

"No, Mo Sholas. Nobody survived that fight. The keep is safe for now."

*For now.* My favorite kind of reassurance.

Still, I nod, glossing over the nickname that he gave me.

He gives me the tour of the castle, throughout which he ignores my frequent Beauty and the Beast references, though he does chuckle at my stolen joke about the Baroque period and my genuine excitement over the library.

I follow him outside, blinking against the brightness. The air is crisp and sharp, filled with the scent of pine and something wilder—like the earth itself is alive. Below the ridge, I see people—shifters, I guess—completing every day tasks.

When we step onto the path, a few heads turn. Conversations stop. I feel their eyes on me—curious, wary, maybe even hostile.

I lean closer to Casimir and mutter, "They don't look thrilled to see me."

"They are surprised," he says carefully.

"Uh-huh. Because nothing screams 'welcome to the neighborhood' like suspicious glares."

His mouth curves slightly. "You're handling this well."

"Is that sarcasm or a compliment?"

"Both."

We reach a wider clearing where a tall woman with sharp cheekbones and a scar along her jaw steps forward. Her presence radiates authority. "Casimir," she greets, then turns her gaze to me. "And this must be the human."

I can't help it—I straighten. "Freya. The human has a name."

Her lips twitch, just barely. "Freya, then. I am Gemma, Caz's cousin. I heard what happened." Her eyes flick to Casimir. "And what you did."

He gives a short nod, jaw tight.

Gemma studies me for a long, unnerving moment before saying, "No one in our clan has ever bonded outside the species before. You've made things...interesting."

I sigh. "That's me. A walking complication."

Casimir makes a low sound—half growl, half warning—and Gemma's eyes flash in amusement. "She has spirit. I like her."

"Don't encourage her," Casimir mutters.

I grin, despite myself. "Too late."

Gemma's expression softens a little. "You'll need time to adjust. We'll do what we can to help. But not everyone will be pleased. Some see the bond between human and shifter as unnatural."

I sigh, rolling my eyes. "Great. Love a good existential controversy first thing in the morning."

Casimir shoots me a look that says *please stop antagonizing her*, but honestly, if sarcasm keeps me from melting down, I'm counting it as a coping mechanism.

Gemma dismisses us after a few more pleasantries, which I find hilarious since Casimir is supposedly the Chief, and we head back toward the castle.

When we reach the steps, Casimir pauses. "You did well."

"By not fainting?"

"By not running," he says quietly.

"Oh, I considered it," I admit. "But I don't know where the hell I am, and you're the only one who can explain why I can now understand bear people."

He huffs a laugh, low and rough. "Fair enough."

We stand there for a moment, just watching each other. The silence stretches, but it's not uncomfortable. His heartbeat hums faintly in my chest, steady and grounding.

And even though I still don't understand this bond, this place, this *everything*, I feel something I haven't felt in a long time.

Hope.

# 7

## Space? Stay.

Casimir

Giving her space is harder than facing down a rebel war-band.

I've faced claws, fire, and fangs. I've bled, buried brothers, and carried the weight of a clan too small and too stubborn to die. None of that prepared me for this. For sitting in silence, pretending that the reason my chest aches is not because the female bound to my heart doesn't want me near her.

Except that is not true. Not exactly.

She never said that she does not want me. She asked for space. She needs time.

And after what she has been through—ripped from her world, nearly killed by those feral bastards, bonded to me without choice. It is no wonder she is wary. Anyone would be.

If only knowing that would stop the quiet spiral in my mind. The part of me whispering that the distance means rejection. That she looks at me and sees only the male who took her choice away. My bear roars at me to fix it, but he does not offer any ideas as to how.

The day after our walk through the keep, I do what I can to keep my distance. I throw myself into chores, into checking the perimeter, into pretending I am not listening for the sound of her voice or for her scent to flow through the halls as she seeks me out.

Every laugh that she offers Gemma or Kiran fills me with longing. My only respite is the feel of her heartbeat in my chest. The bond, reminding me that she is alive and we are tethered.

Dinner is…tense.

Freya sits beside me at the head of the table, because that is her rightful place as Heart Mate of the Chief. But tradition also demands many things of us as a bonded pair that we did not follow leading up to our bonding. Adding in that she is not a bear shifter, has made the energy in the room to turn volatile. The looks that she is getting from some could freeze running water.

Gemma tries to keep order, but the whispers ripple through the room like static—soft, sharp, and cruel. I hear words like *unnatural* and *rushed.* And then someone brings up *the heat.*

My cousins, thankfully, are the only ones who do not act like they have been personally offended by her existence. Bran makes her laugh. Gemma fills her plate like an older sister would. And Kiran, goddess bless him, threatens to accidentally spill stew on anyone who glares too long.

Freya, for her part, is outwardly unshaken. She meets every stare head-on, her humor dry and perfectly timed. The heartbeat I feel in my chest betrays her bravado, but I would never let on. When one of the disapproving bears mutters about her "not looking like much of a Heart Mate," she smiles sweetly, pretends to look in a pocket, and says, "Oops, I must have forgotten my fucks in the other dimension because I don't have any left to give you."

Half of the table goes quiet. Bran chokes on his drink. I try not to laugh, but fail.

Still, by the end of the meal, my patience is hanging on by a thread. When the talk of our missed heat turns from speculation to crude jokes, I growl—a sound that silences the room instantly.

"Enough," I say, my voice low and even. "Freya is under my protection. She is my Heart Mate and she is a part of this clan now."

No one argues, but the looks they give her on the way out makes it clear they do not all accept it. Not yet.

When we return to my quarters, the firelight paints her in gold. She's quiet, thoughtful. Then she turns to me and says, "Casimir, can I ask you something?"

Her tone is hesitant, like she is not sure she wants the answer.

"Of course," I say.

She lets out a steadying breath before bringing her eyes up to meet my own. "What, exactly, is a heat?"

The question hits like a hammer to the sternum. I blink, trying to choose my words carefully. "It's…a time after bonding. Our instincts—our bodies—make demands of…completion. It is a time when fertility peaks. It is not something that is easily ignored."

Her eyes narrow. "So, it's like magically induced lust?"

I wince. "In less crude terms, yes. It is painful to resist, but it can be managed if necessary."

She nods slowly, then looks away. "And it didn't happen with us because…"

I shake my head. "I do not know. But I would guess that it is because the bond formed in desperation, not ceremony. Your body was not strong enough to withstand the demands of a heat."

Her shoulders stiffen. "So, it might still happen."

"It might. I have read about delayed heats due to medical necessity. They usually return in time with the female's natural cycle or with the cycle of bonding suns."

Freya is silent for a long time. When she finally speaks, her voice is small but steady. "If it does, I'm not going to force you into anything. You already did enough when you bonded with me. I won't make you—" she swallows, heart hammering, "—-help me, just because magic says so."

The words hit me like claws across my chest.

"Freya," I start, but she cuts me off.

"I mean it. I would rather suffer through whatever pain comes than go through something that would mean nothing to you. The pity? That would destroy me. I can't use you like that, Casimir."

I do not realize I've moved until I'm standing in front of her. "That's not what this is," I say, my voice rough. "You think I regret saving you? That I do not *want* you? Goddess, Freya, that is not it at all."

She blinks up at me, confusion flickering across her face. "But I thought..."

"I regret that I could not offer you a *choice*," I admit. "That I took your future and bound it to mine without asking. That was a decision that you should have been able to make, and I am so sorry that I stole that from you. But, Freya, I could never regret that it is *you*. Never that."

Her lips part slightly, but no words come out. The air between us hums, that same faint pull in my chest tightening.

After a moment, I force myself to step back. "We'll have time before the heat comes. *If* it comes. You do not need to worry."

She nods, and I can see the thoughts spinning behind her eyes.

I show her how to use the bath next, walking her through the levers and valves. She admitted that she was embarrassed to ask and has been using the cold water to bathe with. I internally berate myself for not thinking to show her sooner.

"It might take a moment to warm up for you," I explain.

"Story of my life," she mutters.

I manage a smile. "I'll be in the next room if you need me."

Leaving her there is a test of will. I sit by the fire, trying to focus on the rhythmic crackle of the flames instead of the faint sound of water and her voice humming softly— some tune I do not know but somehow recognize, like I have heard it before in my dreams.

Then I hear the thud.

I'm moving before I can think.

The door flies open, and she's on the floor—naked, wet, startled. My heart stops.

"Freya!"

"I'm fine," she says quickly, mortified. Her cheeks burn red as she scrambles to cover herself—except there is suddenly fabric shimmering over her skin, appearing out of thin air like a golden smoke condensing into form.

We both freeze.

Then, just as suddenly, the fabric vanishes again, leaving her bare and me speechless.

"What—" I start, but she looks ready to sink through the floor.

Snapping out of it, I grab a towel from the rack and kneel beside her, wrapping it gently around her shoulders. "You're okay," I murmur, just as much for my sake as hers. "Did you hit your head?"

She shakes her head, eyes wide.

"Good." I help her stand, steadying her with one arm. She's trembling—not from cold but from the shock of what just happened.

Magic, wild and unbound. Hers.

We do not speak of it as we finish getting ready for bed. I find her one of my shirts, soft and worn, and she slips it on wordlessly while I strip down to just my pants. The air between us feels charged, fragile.

I reach for the door, meaning to give her space again, when she whispers a single word that stops me in my tracks.

"Stay."

I turn to look at her, feet still frozen to my spot.

"Just, stay. Please."

The word *please* undoes me.

I nod, crossing back to the bed. I slowly lower myself onto the mattress, remaining on top of the blankets. Close enough that I can hear her breathing but far enough that she will not feel cornered or intimidated by my presence.

The bond settles further between us, steady and warm. Her heartbeat hums in my chest against mine—two beats, one cadence.

And as sleep edges closer, I realize that giving her space does not mean stepping away.

It means being there when she is ready to close the distance.

# 8

## The Prophecy & The Scrolls

Freya

When I wake, I'm cocooned in warmth.

For a second, I think I've finally made it to the afterlife—some cozy, cedar-scented heaven with soft bedding and the sound of crackling fire. Then the weight of an arm draped over my waist shifts, and I freeze.

Oh. Right. Not heaven. Not dead. Just bonded for eternity to a giant bear man in a magical mountain forest castle that's half okay with my existence.

Totally normal Tuesday.

Casimir stirs behind me, his breath brushing my neck. His heartbeat—our heartbeat—thuds in sync, steady and annoyingly comforting. I should move. I should absolutely move. Instead, I lie there, memorizing the rhythm.

When I finally peel myself away, he wakes instantly. Of course he does. Apparently, heightened senses come with the whole shifter package.

"Morning," he says, voice rough with sleep.

"Barely," I mumble, rubbing my eyes. "Is this what heaven feels like? Because I expected more clouds and fewer awkward sleepovers."

His mouth twitches, that almost-smile that feels like sunrise. In that moment, my traitorous heart decides that we want all of his smiles.

"Did you sleep at all?"

"Some. I had dreams." I hesitate, then add, "Weird ones."

"About your world?" The crease between his brows deepens and I have to stop myself from reaching out to smooth it.

"About both," I admit. "Chicago and this place sort of crashed into each other. My studio was full of mountains and trees. The paint on my canvases moved." I try for humor. "I think my subconscious needs therapy."

He studies me quietly, eyes searching. "You did something last night. The clothing that appeared…"

"Yeah." I look down at my chest, half-expecting it to spark instead of seeing the simmering glow being emitted from the golden starburst mark. "That was new. Unless I've secretly been a magician all along, which, considering my track record with IKEA furniture assembly, feels unlikely."

Casimir chuckles under his breath, apparently understanding enough of my joke despite never experiencing the literal hell that is reading those instructions.

"Magic does not usually manifest like that. Though, your presence in this world is a bit of a mystery as well. You said that humans do not have magic?"

"Nope. There is not any magic from the world that I came from. Though this—" I say, gesturing to the golden mark on my chest, "—is new too. Maybe it is all connected? Could it be because of our bond?"

He nods slowly, rising from the bed and pacing toward the table where a candle smolders from last night. "Bonded pairs can share abilities. But conjuring is rare. It is not something that I can do, nor is it the magic of my family line. It is most likely connected to the magic of being Sun Kissed." He pauses his pacing, standing right in front of me as he gently brushes his finger against my mark.

"Lucky me," I say breathlessly. "Maybe next time I'll summon some whiskey."

The bond hums faintly between us, warm and alive. It feels different this morning—like the connection has deepened overnight. It is stronger. More present.

I don't mention it.

Because I still don't know what to do with the fact that his heartbeat feels like home, or that the man who saved me looks at me like he's trying not to want something he already does.

I clear my throat. "So, hypothetically—if I keep, uh, flickering like that—does that mean I'm some kind of hazard? Because I am already stirring the pot by being here and now I have this weird power and it just feels like this is probably another neon pink arrow pointing at me to tell others that I'm different."

His brow furrows. "No. It means your magic is evolving. Your body is adapting to this world."

"Evolving," I echo. "Like a Pokémon."

He blinks. "A what?"

"Never mind." I sigh. "Basically, you're saying I'm changing."

"Yes." His gaze meets mine, steady and sincere. "And I do not want you to face that alone. I am here for you, Mo Sholas."

*Mo Sholas.* My Light. My Comfort. My Joy. The translation washes through my mind as something softens in my chest, steady and sincere. I want to tell him I believe him. That I'm starting to understand he didn't regret me, just the lack of choice. But the words get tangled somewhere between my heart and my throat.

Before I can answer, there's a knock at the door.

Casimir tenses, the shift in him immediate—shoulders straight, senses sharp. He crosses the room and opens the door to reveal Kiran. He hands Casimir a small, sealed parchment.

"This just arrived from Callum. It is marked as urgent."

Casimir thanks him, then shuts the door. His expression goes carefully neutral as he breaks the seal. I sit up, instinctively wary.

"What's wrong?"

He scans the letter once. Then twice. His eyes darken. "It's happening."

"What is happening?"

"The prophecy," he says quietly. "Come with me."

I take Casimir's outstretched hand and follow him out of our room, through the quiet halls of the keep, all of the way into the deep underbelly of his home. He pauses before an old, stone door. "Clan Paw is the keeper of the Sun Kissed Scrolls," he explains. "We protect the ancient knowledge of bearkind, the wisdom of our elders, and the prophecies as told by the goddesses."

The stone creaks as Casimir muscles it open, pausing to light candles to illuminate the chamber. Shelves line the walls, each one loaded with books and papers, tools, and gold. I can *feel* the magic as if it is a living being standing with us, surrounding us, accepting us into its home.

"There is a prophecy that speaks of the greed that has corrupted the territory. It speaks of being aided by Sister's Might. You, being blessed as Sun Kissed, are considered a Sister. Just as The Sun is a sister to The Mother—the land. Callum is a Clan Chief from one of the three remaining Sun Kissed lines, like me. His message was a request for aid, stating that the rebels are becoming too powerful, too great in numbers. He wrote of a poem that his cousin, a story keeper, remembered. A way to rid the land of its pain. He is speaking of this prophecy."

Casimir gently shifts through some parchments before he finds the one that he is looking for. I tuck closer to his side, looking at the parchment as he reads it to me.

"It says:

Symptoms of The Mother Cursed<br>
With Rapacity's Blight<br>
There will be Three Sons of the First<br>
Aided by a Sister's Might<br>
Who will Rise from the Shadows<br>
Back into the Light<br>
Together as One<br>
Claw, Paw, and Maw<br>
Will Fight the Bane<br>
Will Start their Reign<br>
And Rid The Mother of her Pain."

My stomach drops. "Well, that sounds fun," I mutter.

"This mark," he says as he brushes his knuckles over my sternum, "Is the mark of the Sun Kissed. All of the females in my family line had one, going as far back as the original Sun Kissed blessing. It is magic that is passed down to each Sister within the line. My family line had the ability to wield sunlight into weapons. Other lines, like Callum's family line had the ability to receive prophetic visions. I believe that your ability to conjure is your magic that you received from The Sun."

I laugh, but it's hollow. "So, I'm not just a cosmic joke. I'm a cosmic *prophecy* now. Fantastic."

Casimir doesn't smile. He looks like the ground just shifted beneath him. "If this is true, Freya, you're not just bonded to me. You're the key to something larger. Something that could change everything."

Great. No pressure.

My first instinct is to deny it. I'm an artist, not a savior. My last masterpiece was a painting of a pigeon wearing a crown. I am *not* chosen-one material.

But then I remember the light under my skin. The clothes that materialized out of thin air. The way that I was brought to this world. The blinding light that I followed. The way that, despite my confusion, I have never felt out of place at Casimir's side. He has always felt like home. Is it possible that I was always meant to be here, in this world, to fulfill this prophecy?

I rub my temples. "Okay. Let's pretend I believe this prophecy stuff. Why would the universe pick *me*? I'm not powerful, or special, or even coordinated enough to stand in a bathtub without almost dying."

Casimir's voice softens. "Maybe because you *are* human. Because you feel deeply. Because you have already survived what should have killed you. That is a strength that those of this world do not possess."

I meet his gaze, and there's something in it that steals the air from my lungs. Something like faith.

I want to tell him not to look at me like that. That I'm terrified. That I'm not ready to carry whatever fate has dumped on my doorstep.

Instead, I say, "So, what now?"

He folds the letter carefully, as if it's alive. "There is more," Casimir tells me quietly. "Cal does not just request aid. He says that he has found his Heart Mate, a human, who was brought here from another world bearing the Sun Kissed mark and has the power to wield incredible magic."

"Like me?"

He nods. "Like you."

I take a deep breath. "But I don't know anything about this magic. I can't help if I don't know how to control it."

"So we learn," he says with a smile and a shrug, as if it is that easy.

"We, huh?"

His mouth curves faintly. "You think I'd let you face this alone?"

"No," I say softly, "but part of me thought you might want to."

He reaches for my hand, pressing it to his chest where I can feel our heartbeat thumping in his chest. The way that his hand engulfs mine, protecting me in such a small but significant way, sends a pulse of heat through my body like a live wire. "Never that."

The world feels too big and strange—but for the first time since I woke up in this place, I don't feel lost.

Because whatever this prophecy means, whatever this magic inside me becomes, I won't be facing it alone. And maybe that is enough.

# 9

## Magic Lessons & Attempted Murder

Freya

Magic, as it turns out, is a lot less "abracadabra" and a lot more *try really hard not to embarrass yourself while your hot situationship stares at you.*

We've been at this for days.

Casimir sits across from me on the floor of our quarters, one knee bent, forearms resting on his thighs—casual, composed, infuriatingly calm. I, on the other hand, look like a cross between a malfunctioning stage magician and someone about to have a nervous breakdown.

"Okay," I mutter, glaring at the small wooden cup between us. "I just want to duplicate it. Copy. Paste. Even just a flicker. I'm not picky. Easy peasy."

Nothing happens.

Casimir's lips twitch. "Maybe try not to glare at it like you plan to murder it."

"I *am* planning to murder it," I grumble.

He exhales a laugh, low, warm, and annoyingly sexy. "Magic will not answer anger. It answers intent."

"I *intend* to make a copy and then murder the original."

He barks out a laugh, wiping a tear from his eye before calming down enough to continue doling out his sage wisdom on controlling magic that he has zero experience with. "You are thinking too hard."

I slump back onto my palms, staring at the ceiling. "You realize that's like telling a drowning person to 'just swim.'"

We've tried everything—meditation, visualization, even Casimir's admittedly very serious attempt at chanting old bear clan words that sounded suspiciously like gibberish written by a poet. Still, nothing. No blasting glow, no flicker, no magic.

It's frustrating. Especially when I *know* the power is there, simmering beneath my skin like a trapped spark.

Finally, I throw my hands up. "Maybe I just need to almost die again. That seemed to do the trick last time."

Casimir's head snaps up, expression sharp. "Don't joke about that."

I blink, startled by the sudden edge in his voice. "I was kidding."

"I know," he says, quieter now, running a hand through his hair. "I just—don't."

The air between us softens. I nod, feeling a little guilty, then sit back up. "Okay. No more death jokes. But clearly, there's a pattern. The only times something happened were when I *really* needed it to."

He frowns thoughtfully. "When you were uncomfortable."

"Right." I groan. "So what, my magic feeds on emotional instability? Great. That's healthy."

He leans forward slightly. "What were you feeling exactly, before it happened?"

My stomach twists. I look anywhere but at him. "I don't know. It was just instinct. Need. I wanted to cover myself. I was embarrassed."

"Why?"

I blink at him. "Why?"

He nods, waiting.

"I mean, I was naked on the floor, floundering in a puddle of bathwater because my brain couldn't communicate with my feet that wet stones are slippery, so—" I say dryly. "That's usually enough reason."

"But why did you *want* to? Why did you *need* to?"

He's too perceptive for his own good.

I sigh, fiddling with the edge of the blanket beneath me. "I was thinking that next to you, I look average. You're built like a damn mountain, and I'm, well, somewhere between soft hills and gently rolling terrain."

His brow furrows. "You think you're not—" He cuts himself off, like he can't even say it. "Freya."

Oh no. He says my name like it's a prayer, and I'm not emotionally prepared for that.

"I'm not fishing for compliments," I add quickly, holding up a hand. "It's just—years of conditioning, okay? My parents, especially my mom, were big on appearances. Perfection. Thin, polished, presentable. And I—" I gesture vaguely to my midsection. "—I like pie too much for that."

Casimir just stares at me, jaw tightening.

Then, slowly, he says, "You think I care about that?"

"I don't know. But even if you don't, it doesn't magically erase years of hearing that I should be less."

He kneels in front of me, moving so close I can feel his heat.

"Freya," he says again, voice low. "You're perfect."

I laugh weakly. "You're biased."

"I am," he agrees, eyes steady on mine. "But that does not make it untrue."

His gaze drifts down, reverent and slow—not predatory, not possessive, but *appreciative*. "Your curves," he says softly, "would fit my hands like they were made for them. The way your body moves—it is powered by strength, not flaw. When you smile, when you paint the air with your words, when you look at me, that's what draws me."

My heart stumbles in my chest. "You—"

He doesn't stop. "Your stomach," he continues, voice roughening, "is soft and warm, and I think about what it would feel like under my palm. Your thighs—"

"Okay," I say quickly, trying not to combust. "I get it. You've got a thing for thick thighs."

He huffs a quiet laugh. "I have a thing for *you*. All of you. You are not less than me, Freya. You never were."

It's too much—his sincerity, the way his voice breaks a little at the end. I try to deflect with a joke, but the words won't come.

"Your mother was wrong," he adds softly. "And anyone who ever made you feel like you had to shrink to be worthy of love—they were blind."

The breath I didn't realize I was holding leaves in a shaky rush.

"Casimir," I whisper.

He reaches up, brushing a thumb across my cheek. "When I look at you, I see the most beautiful being I have ever known. Inside and out."

And somehow, I believe him.

The air hums. My skin prickles. And then—the magic stirs.

It's faint, but real. A shimmer of light from my chest, a flicker like sunlight through leaves. It fades quickly, but it's enough to make both of us freeze.

"You did it," he murmurs, awed.

I stare at the faint afterglow. "Guess I just needed a pep talk from a sexy bear man."

He laughs, shaking his head. "You needed to believe in yourself—in your power."

We stay like that for a while, just breathing in the shared quiet. Then, with a smile tugging at his mouth, he asks, "What about me?"

"What about you?"

"Would you change anything?"

I blink, taken off guard. "You mean, your body?"

He nods, casual but intent.

My brain short-circuits. "Uh, no. Absolutely not. You're...I mean, you're basically sculpted out of granite and good intentions."

He laughs, that deep rumble that hits somewhere low in my stomach. "So, perfect?"

I roll my eyes. "If I say yes, will your ego grow fur and take over the room?"

But my voice softens as I add, "Yeah. Perfect. Exactly what I'd see if I ever let myself imagine what I wanted."

Something in his expression shifts—like he wasn't expecting honesty, and it hit him straight in the heart.

He reaches for my hand again, fingers brushing mine. "It's the same for me," he says quietly. "Exactly."

That night, we lay side by side, like we always do now. No walls. No distance. Just quiet breathing and the shared rhythm of our hearts.

I stare at the ceiling, the bond warm and steady inside me, and let myself think something dangerous.

That maybe—just maybe—I'm falling for him.

I don't know if it's me or the bond. If it's real or magic or both. But for now, it feels real enough.

And for the first time in a long time, I fall asleep feeling more *whole* than I ever did in my old world.

For the next week, magic practice becomes our new normal.

We start small—stones, utensils, the occasional frustrated sigh when I accidentally make a spoon disappear. Then bigger things. Shapes. Colors. Even movement.

The more control I gain, the more I can hold the illusions, stretching time and space with effort. From seconds to minutes. From inches to yards.

Casimir keeps notes—meticulous, detailed, endlessly patient. I keep jokes. Mostly about things that he has no frame of reference for, but he laughs anyway.

Somewhere between the laughter, the sparks, and the moments when his hand lingers a little too long against mine, I realize something terrifying.

I don't just want to learn this magic.

I want *him.*

And that, more than any prophecy or power, might be the most dangerous thing of all.

# 10

## Kiss Me

Casimir

It has been nearly two weeks since Freya first made clothing solidify from shimmering, golden light to cover her bare skin, and I swear the memory still lives under mine.

Every day since, she has grown stronger. More confident. The woman who once shook in my arms from pain now stands before me, hands outstretched, brow furrowed in concentration as a perfect illusion of a wildflower blooms in the air between us.

It flickers. Wavers. Then dissolves into golden dust.

She groans, dropping her hands. "Well, it's a start. A very flimsy start."

I cannot help it, my chest warms with pride. "It lasted longer than yesterday."

She huffs, brushing a strand of hair from her face. "You say that like it's a medal-worthy achievement."

"It is," I remind her. "To my knowledge, there is no other in this entire world that can make images appear out of sunlight. Nobody but you."

Freya rolls her eyes, but she's smiling. She does not see herself the way I do. She does not realize how miraculous it is that she is still standing, still laughing, still trying after everything that she has endured, both in this world and her own.

Her persistence humbles me.

She is the most *real* thing I have ever known, and yet, somehow, she is magic itself.

Every day, I find new reasons to be in awe of her.

Every night, I wrestle with my bear—the primal side of me that growls and paces and demands what he believes is already his.

It is not subtle, that part of me. It wants to finish the bond—to seal it, body and soul. It wants her scent all over me, with mine dripping from her. It wants her heartbeat pressed against mine without space between.

And the most difficult part? I want it too.

But I cannot have it.

Not yet.

She didn't get the chance to choose this bond. I made that choice for her when she was dying in my arms and I refused to risk losing her.

It saved her life.

But it also stole her freedom

So, I wait.

I keep a firm hold of my instincts, even when they snarl at the restraint. Even when she laughs and looks up at me with that quick, brilliant smile that makes something inside me unravel.

Even when she falls asleep in my bed, warm and soft and only inches away.

Because if she ever comes to me, I want it to be her choice. Not magic. Not fate.

Her.

Kiran finds me outside the training hall later that afternoon, ridding myself of pent-up energy.

"Still brooding?" he asks, dropping onto the bench beside me. "You've got that look. The one that usually precedes bad decisions or confessions of unrequited love."

I grunt. "Do not start."

He grins. "Oh, it is definitely love, then."

I glare, but he is immune to it. Always has been.

Kiran leans back, stretching his long legs out. "You could just tell her, you know. Might save the rest of us from watching you suffer in silence."

"She does not need the pressure," I say. "Not when she is still finding her place here."

His smirk fades at that. "About that...some of the clan are still uneasy."

I sit down, my jaw tightening. "Uneasy about what?"

"You know what," he says quietly. "They think the bond is not complete. That because there were no witnessed ceremony, no heat—"

"They think it's not real?" I finish, voice flat.

Kiran sighs. "They are scared, Caz. A human Heart Mate. One from another world. It threatens the order they have lived by for centuries. They have heard the rumors coming from over in the wolf territory, of human women siphoning magic from the packs. *We* believe those rumors to be false, given the True Mate, Moon Touched bonds between the humans and the Alphas. But, when people are scared, they doubt.

"They can doubt all they want," I growl. "It changes nothing."

"Maybe not for you. But you are Chief, Caz. You cannot ignore their concerns."

He is right. I hate that he is right.

The weight of leadership is a familiar burden, but this is different. My bond, my heart, my Mate—these are not matters for council discussion or clan approval. Heart Mate bonds and Sun Kissed blessings are sacred.

I can feel her. Every heartbeat, every flicker of emotion through our connection. My bear recognizes her. My soul recognizes her. She is *mine*.

And how we choose to proceed is not something that is up for debate from anyone outside of the two of us.

Still, I know the whispers will grow if I do not end them.

"I will address it," I say finally.

Kiran nods, satisfied. "Good. And Caz?"

I look at him.

"She is special. You know that. Maybe her presence in this world is not just about the prophecy or her power. Maybe it is about change."

"Maybe," I murmur, staring toward my quarters where Freya is no doubt making something appear—or possibly disappear. "But change is dangerous."

"So is love," Kiran says with a grin, standing. "And you have never been one to back down from danger."

That evening, the clan gathers for dinner. Firelight flickers off stone walls, filling the room with warmth and noise. I sit at the head of the long table, watching as heads bow and laughter rises.

Freya sits beside me, unbothered by the tension threading through the room. I have kept most of the concerns about her place in my world away from her, but she must see the eyes that follow her.

When the noise quiets, I stand.

"Some of you have questions," I begin, my voice carrying easily through the room. "About me. About her." I look down to my Mate, willing her to see the affection in my eyes as silence ripples around us.

"Some of you believe that the bond my Mate and I share is not true because it was not witnessed. Because there was no ceremony, no heat, no spectacle." My tone hardens. "You think the bond between a bear and a human cannot exist."

I let my gaze sweep the room. No one meets it.

"Then hear this," I continue, every word sharp as steel. "When I bonded with Freya, I did it not for glory or recognition, but because my heart sang in her presence. Because my heart called to her, and she answered. I can feel her in my chest. I hear her heartbeat in my own. If you think that is something false or incomplete, then you know nothing of what it means to be Paw."

A low murmur runs through the room.

I slam my hand down on the table, the sound cracking like thunder. "And if any of you believe I am lying—if you doubt my word, my bond, or my right to lead—then challenge me now."

No one moves.

Not a breath, not a whisper.

I let the silence stretch, the weight of it pressing down until even the fire seems to dim.

Then, quietly: "That is what I thought."

I sit back down. The tension ebbs. Freya stares at me, wide eyed, like she has never seen me as anything other than gentle before.

But she should know, I will burn the world before I let anyone question her place at my side.

Later, when the hall has emptied and the moon spills through our window, she turns to me.

"Casimir?"

I glance at her. "Hmm?"

She is standing by the bed, nervous but determined, her fingers twisting in the hem of her shirt. "Kiss me."

I freeze. "Freya..."

Her eyes meet mine, steady. "I've wanted to for a while. I just didn't know if it was me or the bond. But tonight, when you stood up for us like that, I knew. It's both. And I'm done pretending I don't want it."

My pulse roars in my ears. My bear growls approval, pacing beneath my skin.

I cross the space between us slowly, giving her time to stop me if she wants. But she doesn't.

When I finally touch her, it's careful, like admiration, not conquest.

Her breath catches. Mine breaks.

And when our lips meet, it feels like something that has been waiting for lifetimes to happen.

# 11

## Take Me to Pound Town



When his lips touch mine, the world stops.

There's no hesitation, no sharp intake of surprise, no distance left to cross. Only the startling, impossible rightness of it. Like the air has been waiting for this moment too, holding its breath right alongside us.

Casimir kisses me as if he's afraid I'll break, even though we both know I'm not fragile anymore. His mouth moves over mine with admiration. Every brush of his tongue tells me that he has wanted this but was waiting for me to decide.

It's soft at first, a question he asks without words. I answer with my hands clutching his shoulders, with the trembling 'yes' that he swallows from my mouth.

And the bond, the golden string that ties us together, hums like the soft vibrations of a guitar chord. It is not a spark this time, but a deep, steady force that spreads through my chest, warm and certain. I can feel our heartbeats in perfect sync, beating together, completely as one.

For so long, I've held myself back.

Afraid that what I felt wasn't me, that it was just some magical tether confusing my heart. But after tonight, after seeing him stand before his clan, voice steady and proud as he defended *us*, I now know better.

It doesn't matter if magic played a part. Because what I feel right now isn't an enchantment. It's a choice.

I need him like I need air. Like I've been holding my breath for too long and he's the first clean inhale.

His hand finds the small of my back, pulling me closer until I can feel the heat of his body seep into mine. When his forehead rests against mine, his breath ragged and uneven, he whispers, "Tell me to stop."

"Don't you dare."

Something flickers in his eyes, relief, want, something achingly tender, and then he kisses me again, deeper this time. I melt against him, the sound of my name on his lips sinking straight to my core.

Time blurs. The kiss turns from gentle to consuming, but never harsh.

When we finally break apart, we're both breathing hard, and my hands are fisted against his chest like I'm afraid he'll disappear.

He doesn't.

Instead, he gathers me against him, wrapping me in his arms until my head rests over his heart. I let myself sink into it. The warmth, the safety, the unspoken promise that's always existed between us.

"Sleep," he murmurs, brushing his lips over my temple.

And I do.

For the first time since waking in this strange world, I sleep without nightmares. No broken glass. No blood. No fading memories of the life I lost.

Only sunlight.

Only his voice, low and steady in my dreams.

Only peace.

When I wake hours later, something is wrong.

My body feels feverish. Heat rolls under my skin, sharp and pulsing, like fire chasing through my veins. My shirt clings to me, damp with sweat, and my heart is beating too fast.

Casimir isn't beside me.

The panic comes then, sharp and immediate, until I hear his voice, speaking in hushed tones near the door.

Gemma's voice answers, quick and anxious. I can't make out every word, but I hear my name.

"Casimir?" I whisper, throat dry.

He turns immediately, his expression shifting from tense to soft in an instant. He's at my side before I can blink, kneeling beside the bed, his hand finding mine.

"Freya," he murmurs, voice thick with concern. "I'm here."

A whimper leaves my chest. "I don't feel good," I tell him. "What's...what's happening to me?" My skin feels like it's burning, but I'm not cold or sick. There is just a dizzy, overwhelming ache.

He hesitates, brushing a strand of hair from my forehead. "I think you are going into heat, sweetheart."

The words barely register. "Heat?"

He nods slowly. "It might just be the right timing with your cycle, or maybe it is because our bond has grown stronger and the kiss we shared set things in motion."

I swallow hard, trying to think through the fog in my mind.

"It is the body's way of sealing the bond completely," he continues, his brow furrowed as I try to breathe through the ache deep in my core. He lifts my hand to his mouth, placing a gentle kiss on my heated skin. "If it runs its course without release, it will be painful."

I blink up at him, dazed. "And how—how does it end?" Somewhere in the back of my mind, I know that we have talked about all of this before, but I can't find the answers through the cloud of pain and overwhelming *need*.

Casimir meets my gaze, no hesitation, only sincerity. "Through intimacy. Our bond will demand completion."

Sex. He is talking about sex. And orgasms. I need so many orgasms. It is the only way I will feel better.

"Yes, my love. You will need orgasms. You will need mine too. Our joint release is what will make the pain go away."

I didn't realize I had said that out loud. The heat in my body spikes, curling low in my stomach. "Oh."

He cups my cheek gently, his voice low but firm. "Freya, listen to me. You do not owe me anything. This is your choice. Always. I can help you manage the pain if you are not ready for this step."

I stare at him, my heart breaking a little at how careful he is with me. How every word is wrapped in restraint.

"I want you," I whisper. "But I don't want you to feel like you *have* to help me."

He exhales, something like relief and hunger tangled in his breath. "There is nothing that I would not share with you. Not my strength. Not my heart. Not my body. You can have it all."

The fire inside me swells, my fingers clutch his wrist. "Then don't make me wait."

His jaw tightens, a low sound rumbling in his chest—the bear, I think. But when he looks at me, it's only Caz. My Caz.

"This is always your choice," he says again.

And when he leans down, when his lips find mine, there's no fear left between us.

Only the bond.

Only the fire.

Only us.

"Please, Caz," I beg, lifting my hips up in search of relief. "I need you."

"Gemma!" he shouts as he brushes his knuckle against my center. "Lock our wing down. Leave food outside the door and have Kiran handle any issues that arise for the next several days."

"Of course, Chief," she says. I can hear the smirk in her tone but I can't muster up the energy to be embarrassed that she has been witness to my needy moans.

The heat comes in waves.

Not just the burning under my skin, but the ache that settles somewhere between my ribs and my heart, demanding his touch.

It's ridiculous, really. I survived heart surgery as a child. I survived my parents and their judgment. I survived a car crash that killed both of my friends. I survived being kidnapped and abused by the rebels in this world. And somehow, this—wanting him—is what threatens to undo me completely.

Caz doesn't rush me. He never does. His hand cups the back of my neck, thumb tracing slow, careful circles like he's coaxing calm into my bones. I can feel the tremor in his fingers, though. He's holding himself together by a thread. Somehow, that makes me want him more.

He is all patience and quiet strength as he touches me like I am made of starlight.

"I feel like I'm on fire," I manage to whisper.

His lips tilt. "You are. You are burning up with need."

"Oh, great. Love that for me," I mutter, pulling a laugh from his chest. The sound rolls through me and makes the air feel heavier.

Then he leans in, and humor dissolves into something else entirely. His mouth meets mine, slow and adoring, like he's asking for permission with every breath.

I should be nervous. Normally, I would be. I would be thinking about the light, the angle, the fact that I'm a human-shaped collection of imperfections.

But not now.

Not with him.

Caz looks at me like I'm art. Like I've already been carved and painted by something divine, and he's just grateful to be allowed to look.

When I reach for him, he slowly rids himself of his pants. My breath catches.

I'd seen him before—technically—when he dragged me half-dead from that cave. But that doesn't count.

Now, though. Fuck, he is perfect.

Caz is all power and restraint, dark skin gleaming like bronze in the flickering light, muscles shifting under every breath. My brain short-circuits somewhere between *admiring artistically* and *please and thank you.*

And his cock? The sight alone makes my mouth water. He is large. Larger than I have ever seen. The head of his cock is swollen and dripping. The bead of cum begging me to taste him. And the piercings…he is pierced through the head with crossed golden bars and has a stud at the base. I have never been with a man who was pierced, but I need to feel those piercings rubbing against my clit and inner walls so badly, it hurts.

"Please, Caz. I need your cock."

He had been fucking me gently with his fingers, stretching me slightly. Offering a small amount of relief. But it isn't enough. When I beg for his cock, he slips his glistening fingers between his lips, sucking me off of his hand and groaning at the taste of me.

He notices me staring and gives me that almost-shy smile that absolutely shouldn't exist on a man like him. "You're sure?" he asks, voice low.

"Completely," I say. Then, because I'm me: "Take me to pound town."

He huffs a laugh, the sound soft against my lips, and moves closer.

When his skin finally touches mine, his cock lined up with my entrance, I stop breathing. The fire in me shifts from chaos to clarity. Every doubt, every scar, every self-conscious thought melts away under the weight of his tenderness.

Caz doesn't touch me like he's taking.

He touches me like he's *listening*.

Every brush of his hands feels like a vow: *I see you. I want you. You're safe.*

And I believe it.

I've never been worshiped before. It makes me want to cry and laugh and curse and thank every god in this world all at once.

Pushing gently at my entrance, my greedy pussy sucks him in. I feel my walls stretch to their limit as they make room for him, the slight discomfort grounding me in the moment, stopping me from floating away.

Taking my mouth with his, he fucks his tongue against mine, swallowing my cries as he pushes himself into me with one long, slow thrust.

"Fuck, Mo Sholas," he moans against my neck. "You feel so fucking good."

Once he is fully seated, he pauses for only a moment before pulling out and thrusting back in, hard. Fast. Exactly what I need. When the piercing at the base of his penis rubs against my clit, I am done for. I scream out my release, shattering into a million little pieces of stardust.

He fucks me through it, lifting my leg to shift positions as he pulls orgasm after orgasm out of me, our bodies slick with sweat and my release, until finally, he roars with his own, shooting his cum deep within me, and calming the heat down to a simmering burn.

When he whispers my name against my skin, it doesn't sound like a word. It sounds like a promise.

The world narrows to the heat between us, the pulse, the breath, the light. And when it finally breaks open, bright and blinding, I realize I am not afraid anymore.

Because this isn't magic pulling the strings.

It's love, blooming in the fire.

# 12

## Well Fed

Casimir

The fire has burned low again.

Three days.

Three nights.

I have lost count of how many times the flames have dwindled to embers only for me to stoke them back to life, both the ones in the hearth and the ones in her.

Freya sleeps now, finally. Her body is soft against mine; her breath is steady. This is the first time in the last three days that she has slept for more than a few minutes, the heat persistent in its demands for release. Even now, she sleeps while impaled on my cock. I can feel as her tight channel squeezes, wanting more but her body is too exhausted to keep up with the demand.

I should rest. I tell myself that each time her breathing evens out, but every time I close my eyes, I find myself wanting to watch her instead.

There is something sacred about her in sleep.

She curls toward my warmth, pressing her face and palm firmly against my chest as if she knows that is where she lives now. Her skin flickers faintly in the firelight, matching the light golden glow pulsing from the Sun Kissed mark resting between the curves of her breasts.

I have fought in battles, led hunts, faced down rival clans while being vastly outnumbered—but nothing has ever undone me the way this woman does by simply existing.

And goddess, I am exhausted.

My body feels like it has been through a thousand battles, and yet, I cannot remember ever feeling so whole.

Day after day, locked in this room, her heat calling to me in waves. I should feel caged, but instead it feels like the world narrowed to exactly what it was always meant to be— just her and me.

I brush a strand of golden hair from her cheek. She murmurs something incoherent and presses closer, her skin still heated.

I have seen her conjure light and shape illusions, but there is more to it than that. When she focuses, it feels as though the world itself holds its breath. I wonder if she could use it to guard the sacred scrolls.

The chamber is hidden, but not invisible. If anyone could weave an illusion strong enough to hide its entrance, it would be her. The thought steadies me, a purpose beyond this war, beyond the prophecy. Something real.

If both Cal and I found our Heart Mates beyond our world, then perhaps Sol will too. The three of us, bound together by the Sun Kissed blessings of our lines, brought back into the light to help fulfill the prophecy? That could make all of the loss that we suffered mean something.

I would wager that Cal has already reached out to Sol for aid as well. When we travel to Claw, I might finally see the threads of this puzzle begin to take shape.

The war that is coming will demand more of us than we have ever given. My clan is small. Too small. Providing aid while maintaining protection over the scrolls will stretch us too thin. But when I look at Freya, at her light, her stubbornness, her fierce heart, I feel something I have not felt in a long time.

Hope.

I rest my forehead against hers, Her skin smells strongly of cherries, almonds, and me. Her pulse is soft but steady beneath my lips. I let out a long breath I did not realize I was holding.

"Thank you," I whisper.

For surviving.

For choosing me.

For proving that even in all of the darkness that has surrounded me since my family was taken from me, something good can still be found.

I pull her a little closer, her curves fitting perfectly against me. The bond hums. Content. Complete.

When the heat has passed, I will think about the journey.

When the heat has passed, I will speak to Kiran, come up with a plan to protect the scrolls and help Cal protect our lands from the rebels.

When the heat has passed, I will be Chief again.

But for now, I am just hers.

And as the fire sinks to quiet embers, I finally let sleep take me—her heartbeat guiding me home.

"Caz." Her whimper drags me from the depths of sleep.

"I am here, Mo Sholas," I reply, capturing her lips with mine as I roll us, sliding out of her wet heat, and hovering my body over top of hers.

Flicking her nipple with my tongue, I rub gentle circles over her aching bundle of nerves above her cunt.

A soft knock at the door alerts me to the food that has just been delivered.

Her body shifts against mine, seeking relief, and the motion nearly undoes me. My bear growls at me, snapping me out of the lust that she has reawakened within me. Discipline returns—barely. "Freya, you need food. Real food."

She groans dramatically. "But you're right here," she says as she grinds her wet heat against my hip. "Delicious. Convenient. Low-prep."

"Low-prep?" I bark out a laugh, genuinely happy that her sense of humor is returning after days lost in a fog. "That is what I am to you now? An easy snack?"

She grins seductively, biting down on her lower lip as her eyes lower to my cock. "A very filling one."

I growl to cover up my amusement, but my laugh breaks through anyway. She has that effect on me. "You have not eaten a proper meal since yesterday," I remind her.

"I don't need food," she insists, trailing her fingers down my body, not stopping until she takes my cock in her hand. "I need you."

"You need both," I reply with a sigh. "The heat has burned through any reserves that you may have had. You will not make it through another round of anything if you faint halfway through."

Freya's eyes narrow. "You drive a hard bargain, Chief."

"Play with your needy pussy while I get our food," I growl into her neck as I pry myself out of her grasp. When I return to the bed, I suck her fingers into my mouth before offering her a plate.

She flops back onto the pillow with a dramatic groan. "Fine," she says as she grabs a hunk of bread and cheese off of the plate. "But only if you eat too." Freya drops her knees to the mattress, spreading herself wide open for me.

I smirk. "Do you need some motivation, my love?"

She nods. "Motivation is important." Her smirk is pure mischief. "You feed me bread and I will feed you honey." Swirling her finger in the honey on her plate, she drags it down her middle, not stopping until she has coated her core in the sticky substance.

I shake my head, trying and failing not to smile. "You are impossible." Lifting the bread with some cheese on it to her mouth, I say, "Bite."

She hesitates just long enough to earn a spanking later, then leans forward and takes it from my fingers, lips brushing the edge of my knuckle. Her eyes gleam with quiet triumph.

"See?" she says around the mouthful. "Compromise."

I chuckle. "You're going to be the death of me."

"Probably," she says, smiling into her cup of water. "But you'll die well-fed."

Once I am sure that she is going to continue eating, I lower my tongue to her body, licking the path of honey from her chest, swirling around the buds of her nipples, down to her navel, taking a moment to nibble at her hips, before covering her thighs with kisses and bites.

I tease. I savor. But I do not give her the attention that she wants until she is practically flying off the bed in search of my tongue. All of my restraint is being tested but I am determined to make her eat as much food as she can so that she restores her strength.

I give her cunt a firm slap as punishment for her impatience but then quickly blow cool air against her clit. She detonates, gushing her arousal, which I gladly devour. She was joking before about me dying between her thighs, but fuck, what a way to go.

Lapping at her center, I fuck my tongue in and out of her before bringing it back up to her clit. I push my thumb inside her pussy, getting it nice and wet before pushing it against her asshole, loving the moan that erupts from her chest at the intrusion.

I discovered early on in the heat that there is not much that she is not willing to try. I have yet to fuck her ass properly. She needs my cum inside her cunt to quell the heat. But that has not stopped me from prepping her for my thick length.

When she has eaten over half of the food on her plate, she sets it to the side, weaving her fingers into my short hair and keeping my tongue pressed firmly where she needs it the most. I pull another orgasm out of her before coming up for air.

"Was I a good girl?" she whimpers as another flare of heat washes over her. "I ate my food."

I bring my lips up to meet hers, her arousal dripping off of my chin. "You were a very good girl, Mo Sholas. What would you like as your reward? Hmm?" I bring my lips to her Mate mark, flicking my tongue over it in a way that I know will cause her immense pleasure.

"I want to choke on your cock," she moans against my neck. "I want you to make me come from fucking my face and then I want you to wreck my pussy with your massive dick. I want your cum so deep inside of me that it will stay forever."

"Fuuuuuuuuck."

I do not know if it is the heat or if it is her growing comfort level with me, but I swear to the goddess that my Mate could make me spill my seed just from the words that she speaks.

She is as dichotomous as our skin. Insecure but confident. Pure but tempting. Honesty breaking through her dry sense of humor.

Climbing up her body, I position the head of my cock against her swollen lips, pausing just long enough to be sure she is ready.

Sliding between her lips, she swirls her tongue, collecting the beads of cum that are already leaking out at just her words. I give her a moment to relax her throat before pushing in further, not stopping until the piercings at the head of my cock makes her gag and moan in succession. This is not the first time that she has taken me into her mouth, and she does not hesitate to swallow me down, lifting her hand to her throat, not in an effort to signal distress but to feel from the outside how deep I reach.

Leaning forward onto my knees, I keep my weight off of her as I use her mouth, just as she asked. I thrust in and out in slow, firm strokes. Her tears and spit making a lovely mess of her face.

I can feel her pressing her thighs together behind me, getting off on being used.

"Are you going to come for me, sweetheart?" I ask through panted breaths, holding my release back so that I do not spill down her throat. "Do you like when I feed you my cock?"

"Mmfmm," she moans around my length, and fuck, the vibration almost sends me over the edge.

"You are doing too good of a job," I say, reaching behind me. "I am going to need you to come now so that I can fill your greedy pussy." Finding what I was reaching for, I pinch her clit, sending her over the edge and quickly pulling my shaft from her mouth as the force of her orgasm causes her to convulse.

"Good girl," I whisper, scraping my teeth against her jaw as I slam my cock into her pulsing cunt, fucking her harder than I ever have before, imprinting her inner walls into the perfect mold of me, and blasting us both into orgasmic bliss.

97

# 13

## Leaking Emotions

Freya

When I wake, the first thing I notice is that I'm not on fire.

No burning under my skin. No restless energy humming in my veins. No sharp pulse demanding more. Just peace. Quiet. Sweet, glorious, bone-deep calm.

The second thing I notice is Caz.

He's sprawled out beside me, blanket tangled around his hips, breathing slow and deep. His arm is flung across his face; the other hand is resting lightly on my hip like his body refuses to stop touching me even in sleep.

And damn, he looks wrecked. In a stupidly unfair, cinematic way—all sharp jaw and shadowed cheekbones, like someone sculpted exhaustion and somehow made it beautiful.

"Pussy: 1, Bear: 0," I snort. Though in all honesty, this poor, magnificent creature was the true star of the show for the last several days. I'm not sure that I could have survived without him.

He doesn't stir, which is good because if he did, I'd probably try to mount him out of habit, and I need to give my vagina a break. I stretch gingerly, and everything in me protests—sore, heavy, but also weirdly good. My limbs feel loose, my magic feels calm.

I run a tentative hand down my side. Still soft. Still flawed. Still me.

But the difference is, I don't care.

All of those little voices from my old world, the ones that told me I had to be smaller, quieter, smoother, prettier—they've finally shut the hell up.

Despite everything that I have put it through, this body has the audacity to feel powerful. And I make a promise to myself that I will never put weight to those negative thoughts again. If it wasn't for my solid frame, I would never have been able to withstand the intensity of the heat. There is no doubt in my mind that my demands would have split me in half if I was the size I always dreamed of being.

"Take that, diet culture," I mutter under my breath.

And that's when the tears start.

They sneak up on me, one second I'm feeling like a victorious goddess, the next my face is leaking uncontrollably. It's ridiculous. I clap my hands over my mouth, trying to muffle the sound, but it is no use. The tears just keep coming.

Hormones, sure. Exhaustion, probably. But it's more than that.

I'm crying because Caz was gentle with me. Because he treated me like I was made of light, not breakable glass. Because for the first time in my entire life, someone touched me without any desire to change me.

I'm crying because I finally know what it means to be chosen. Not for what I could become or what I could provide, but for what I already am. Who I am.

And I'm crying because I want to tell my friends.

I want to tell them everything. About Caz. About the bond and how my life somehow turned into an epic fantasy romance novel with actual emotional depth.

But they are gone. My old world is gone. The old me is gone. And even though I know I am better here, it doesn't soothe the sting of not being able to share this with them.

The sob that breaks out of me us ugly and raw, the kind that shakes your ribs apart and takes all of your breath away.

I bury my face in the blanket, willing myself to stop.

"Freya?" His voice is rough with sleep, warm, and instantly alert. "What is wrong?"

I shake my head, words wobbling. "Nothing. Everything. I don't even know. I'm fine, it's just…"

He props himself up on one elbow, eyes heavy-lidded and full of concern. Then, without another word, he gathers all of my pieces into his arms and holds me together while I fall apart.

I cling to him and cry. For my friends, my world, the person that I used to be. I cry because the heat is over and I'm not ready to go back out into the world with a brave face and the weight of the world resting on my shoulders. I cry because Caz is here and real and holding me like I am something worth keeping.

He doesn't try to shush me or talk me out of it. He just stays. His big hand strokes my back in slow, steady circles. His chest rumbles softly against my ear as he breathes with me until my body finally starts to settle.

When I've cried myself quiet, he presses his lips to my temple. His voice is soft. Careful. "I wanted to tell you something before," he says, hesitating. "But I did not want you to think it was just the heat talking."

I sniff, blinking blearily up at him. "What is it?" I ask. "Do I snore? Because honestly, I think we've passed the point of keeping romantic illusions alive."

He smiles, but his eyes remain steady. Sure. "I love you, Freya."

My brain short-circuits.

"What?" I manage, eloquent as ever.

"I love you," he says again, firmer this time, the words rolling out like a vow. "I should have said it sooner. I should have told you right away when I knew, but I was afraid that I would scare you off. And then, the heat started…But now, I think you really need to know. I love you. I see you. I choose you."

And there it is again, that ache in my chest that's too big to contain.

"Of course you pick *now* to say it," I mutter, my voice breaking halfway through. "When I'm snotty, red-eyed, and emotionally unhinged. This is peak romance, really. Every girl's dream."

His thumb brushes a tear off my cheek. "You do not hide when you are like this. I like it. It is honest."

"You like me blotchy and leaking emotions everywhere?" I sniff. "You're a strange man, Chief."

He chuckles. "Maybe. But I am yours."

The tears well up again, because apparently I'm *that* person now. I laugh through it, shaking my head. "I think you may have suffered a brain trauma."

He laughs quietly. It is my favorite sound in the entire world.

"I love you too," I whisper. The words come out raw and trembling but true. "I think I've loved you longer than I realized. And I think…I think I was meant to find you. To be here. In this world. In your arms."

He exhales, long and slow, and pulls me in so close I can feel our heartbeat as it tries to break out of his chest.

"That is all I need," he murmurs.

Me too.

Outside, the first light of morning spills through the curtains, soft, golden, gentle. The kind of light that makes everything look reborn. I rest my head on Caz's chest, breathing in his scent that has always felt like home.

Maybe I'm still a mess. Maybe I'll cry again in five minutes. Maybe the world is about to end. But right now, I'm exactly where I'm meant to be.

# 14

## Go Out with a Bang

Freya

There is something deeply unfair about the way the world insists on continuing after life-changing revelations.

Like, yes, I cried my soul out, confessed my love, and basically rewrote the entire emotional rule book of my existence. And yet somehow, the universe expects me to put on my big girl pants and go to breakfast like a normal functioning adult.

Minus the pants, of course. I am still just rocking one of Caz's shirts and have zero plans to confine my coochie for the foreseeable future.

By the time Caz and I step out of our room, the sun is already high enough to burn away the fog. The air smells crisp, alive—and it's weirdly comforting. After spending nearly a week sealed inside our bedroom, it feels like stepping into a new world as a completely new woman.

Of course, the actual world that we step into is full of knowing grins.

Gemma is the first to spot us. She's sitting at the long table in the dining hall with a mug of tea and the most dangerous weapon known to womankind: a raised eyebrow.

"Well, well," she says, voice smooth as honey and twice as smug. "Look who decided to rejoin the land of the living."

"Barely," I mutter, brushing imaginary wrinkles from my shirt. "My legs are filing a formal complaint."

Bran, who is sitting across the table, snorts into his drink. "I'd say you've both earned it. Haven't heard the keep that lively in years."

Caz chokes on air. "Bran."

"What?" Bran grins unrepentant. "It's true. I was starting to think you might need some help."

Kiran, sitting beside him, doesn't even look up from his plate. "There is no helping a bonded pair experiencing their first heat."

I decide then and there that breakfast might also be my villain origin story.

"Right," I say, sliding into a seat. "Lovely to see that privacy laws don't exist here."

Gemma hides a laugh behind her mug. "We're a small clan, dear. Sound travels."

"Clearly," I mutter, stabbing a piece of fruit like it personally offended me. "I'll never be able to make eye contact with anyone again."

Caz squeezes my knee under the table, part reassurance, part apology, part *please don't murder my friends before we leave.*

His eyes meet mine, amused and warm. "They are just jealous," he says quietly.

I arch a brow. "Of what? My emotional instability or your stamina?"

Gemma snorts tea through her nose. Bran claps, delighted. "Goddess, I have missed her."

"Do not encourage her," Caz warns.

"Too late," I say sweetly, dramatically batting my eyelashes at him.

The teasing fades slowly into a more serious rhythm as plates are filled and plans start to form. Kiran unrolls a rough map across the table, its parchment worn thin and smudged with ink.

"This is our route south," he says, tapping the mountains. "We'll travel through the hidden tunnels."

Caz nods grimly. "The rebels have not found them. Not yet. But we will need to make sure that they do not see where we enter or exit."

"Which means we leave at dawn," Bran adds. "Low light, fewer patrols, and most of them will be sleeping off a hangover."

Gemma frowns. "And the keep? We cannot leave it unguarded."

My stomach knots. It's strange how this cold, stone fortress has started to feel like home, and now we're about to abandon it.

Caz leans forward, his expression shifting back into command. "We lock it down. Reinforce every gate, seal the inner doors, flood the lower passages. The rebels will not risk breaching stone that deep. They would bring the whole mountain down on their heads before they ever got in."

Kiran nods. "We can trigger the rockfall gates once we're clear. No one gets in or out until we return."

"Good," Bran says. "Because if they get their hands on the scrolls, we will have more than a war on our hands."

I stab another piece of fruit, feeling salty about landing myself in a starring role of a prophecy that no one thought to run past me.

Caz catches my glance, one brow lifting as his silent check in to make sure that I am okay. And even though I am one minor existential crisis away from panic-eating the entire breadbasket, I manage a small nod.

"The scrolls stay in the hidden chamber," Caz says. "We will wall the entrance shut from the inside once they are secured. Even if the rebels find the keep, they will need more than muscle to get through solid granite"

Bran exhales. "That will buy us time."

The room quiets for a beat. Time. The one thing we never seem to have enough of.

I poke absently at my plate, trying to make sense of everything. The prophecy. My role in it. The fact that I, an anxiety-riddled, clumsy, human, am somehow the answer in a shifter war.

*No pressure, Freya. Just carry the fate of an entire species on your emotionally unstable shoulders.*

Caz's hand brushes mine under the table, grounding me instantly.

"We will do it together," he murmurs.

"We don't even know what we are supposed to do yet," I whisper back.

He smiles softly. "There is not anything that we cannot do together. You are so much stronger than you realize."

I roll my eyes, but warmth spreads through me anyway. "Flattery first thing in the morning. That's a dangerous habit to start."

He leans closer. "It is not flattery. It is the truth."

And just like that, I'm smiling again, despite the apocalypse-level weight of the conversation.

The rest of the clan dives into logistics—supply counts, escape routes, signals. I try to follow, but my brain keeps flickering between the enormity of what's coming and the absurdity of this entire situation.

My body still aches from five days of a magical sex fest. I am about to use magic, which I have not fully mastered, to help fulfill a prophecy. And I am sitting here, eating berries in a room full of people who turn into bears, as if it's just another Monday.

By the time we finish, the plan is set. The keep will be sealed by nightfall. We'll leave before sunrise, heading south through the tunnels toward Claw Keep.

As everyone disperses to prepare, I linger near the window, watching light spill across the snow-topped mountain peaks.

Caz steps up behind me, wrapping his arms around my waist. "Are you ready?" he asks softly, kissing my temple.

I lean into him, exhaling. "Define ready."

He chuckles. "Alive, sarcastic, and terrifyingly beautiful?"

"Then yes," I say. "Barely."

He presses another kiss to my shoulder. "That is all I need."

I turn in his arms, meeting his eyes. "You know this journey is going to be chaotic, right? I am not built to be a girl scout. I grew up in a city. I only slept outside before out of pure exhaustion. What if I can't sleep and I need you to entertain me all night?"

A filthy smile pulls at his lips. "I can think of plenty of ways to entertain you all night."

I feel my cheeks heat as I think of what he most likely has in mind. "You can't fuck me in the middle of camp while your clan pretends to not listen."

He gently sucks on his bite mark, sending a bolt of pleasure straight to my traitorous pussy. "You will just have to be a good girl and let me swallow your moans, because this journey will take at least a week and now that I have had a taste, there is nothing that will stop me from drowning in you."

His hand snakes around to my ass, pressing me firmly against his hard cock, leaving zero doubt in my mind that he means every word.

And that, my friends, is how I ended up getting fucked against the dining room window while everyone else in the keep prepared for war.

# 15

## In Full Color

Casimir

The air before dawn has a weight to it. The kind that sits in your lungs and reminds you how alive you are. It is cold enough to bite and still enough that every sound carries.

The keep behind us is silent, sealed. Every gate is reinforced, the inner doors bolted and chained, the tunnels flooded just enough to keep intruders guessing. We have done what we can. What happens next, is on us.

Freya stands beside me, bundled in the warmest cloak I could find, trying to look brave. She is mostly succeeding, except for the way she keeps fidgeting with the strap of her pack and chewing on her lip.

"Are you all right?" I ask quietly.

"If 'all right' means not throwing up from nerves, then yes. Barely."

"I will protect you," I promise her.

The panic in her eyes softens just enough to let me know she believes me.

"I just didn't know that I had a fear of small spaces until you told me we would be crawling through a tunnel full of who-knows-what for *hours*. Based on the size of my apartment back in Chicago, I would have thought I was used to it by now."

Behind us, Bran and Kiran finish checking the packs, while Gemma and the other clan members whisper over the map one last time. The eleven of us, including Freya, move like a practiced machine. It should reassure me. But it doesn't.

If we run into one of the larger rebel clans on the trail, we will be outnumbered. I trust my clan, I know that they would fight to their last breath to protect Freya, but that is the problem. We cannot afford for anyone to take their last breath.

I shove that thought aside and focus on Freya's worries instead. I will keep her close. Keep her laughing.

As we start down the narrow path toward the hidden entrance, she glances up at me. "So," she says, "if I die in this tunnel, I want it on record that this was a terrible idea."

I smirk. "Noted. But you are not dying in a tunnel."

"Good, because that would be embarrassing. 'Here lies Freya: died of claustrophobia and sarcasm.'"

Gemma snorts from ahead. "We will make sure the epitaph rhymes. Maybe add in how good you looked in fur."

Freya sticks out her tongue, earning a few chuckles that ease the tension for a moment. When we reach the mouth of the tunnel, a dark slit in the rock hidden behind an overhang of towering pine, I take her hand. "Stay close," I say. "I am not sure if you gained my ability to see in the dark when we bonded."

'Translation, I'm about to trip over every rock in existence."

"Probably." I grin. "But I will catch you."

The tunnel swallows us whole. It is damp. Echoing. The kind of dark that feels alive. Freya must feel it too because she holds my hand in a death grip, flinching with every drop of water or scrape against the stone.

To distract her, I lean down and murmur, "You know, if you make it through this tunnel without screaming, I will owe you a reward."

Her voice is suspiciously steady. "A reward?"

"Mmm." I pretend to consider. "What would be proper motivation?"

"Stick to your strengths, Chief. You know what will motivate me."

"But I am so good at so many things, Mo Sholas. How to choose just one?"

She snorts. "I think a proper reward should include at least two, maybe three things."

I lower my head, capturing her ear with my teeth. "Is my Mate feeling needy?"

She bites her lip. The tiny moan that escapes vibrates straight through me. "Your Mate is feeling greedy. And she is not at all ashamed to admit it."

"Goddess," Bran mutters. "If they start flirting any louder, the rebels will hear us."

"At least then you could find a female to help you out with your little problem," Kiran teases back, looking pointedly at Bran's cock.

"Walk faster," I growl, and the echo of laughter ripples down the line, soft and quick.

Hours blur together in the dark. The air grows thicker, warmer. Freya stays close, her smaller steps matching mine. When her nerves start to creep back, I keep talking. I tell her about the view we will see when we come out the other side. I talk about how the tunnels were carved generations ago. About the places I will take her when this is over. About the *ways* I will take her once we have an ounce of privacy returned to us.

By the time I see the faint light ahead, her breathing has steadied again. I can feel her pulse. Quick, but no longer panicked.

We listen at the exit. Nothing. No footsteps. No voices. No scent of anyone nearby. Just the calming sound of wind through the trees.

"Looks clear," Gemma whispers.

We slip out one by one, keeping low. The valley beyond stretches wide and green beneath the hot sun. For a moment, none of us move. Just breathe.

I look over to Freya as she lets the sun warm her face. She peels off her cloak, soaking up as much sunlight into her creamy skin as possible. She is beautiful. Breathtaking.

When we are far enough away from the tunnel, I give the signal. The clan strips down without ceremony, shifting in flashes of muscle and fur. It is something that I have seen so many times before, but today I am watching Freya, seeing it from her eyes.

She stands blinking at us, head tilted to the side, half amused, half horrified as skin and hair spread along the growing forms of the bears that live within our skin. Being the last to shift, I let her eyes peruse my body, offering her a wink when she raises her eyes enough to meet my gaze.

There is little I enjoy more than watching as the pale skin of her chest and cheeks flush.

She clears her throat. "You could warn a girl before the spontaneous group nudity."

I laugh, pulling her firmly against my body and devouring her mouth in a firm, languid kiss.

When I pull back, Freya buries her face into my chest.

"You will need to climb up my back after I shift. Hold tight to my fur," I instruct her before delivering one final kiss to her forehead and shifting right in front of her. The world sharpens into scent and sound and instinct as the bear takes over.

Freya approaches carefully, eyes wide. I lower myself flat to the ground so she can climb on.

"You're serious?" she asks.

I chuff a laugh.

"Fine." She grips the thick fur on my leg, using my knee as leverage to boost herself up and onto my back. "But if I fall off, it has everything to do with you being the size of a house and nothing to do with my lack of coordination."

We move south, into the light and warmth. The frozen forest thins. The air softens. The mountains give way to rolling hills and scattered wildflowers. Freya talks the entire journey—to me, to herself, to anyone listening.

She points out colors. The green of new moss. The blue in the river that runs like glass beside us. She tells us about her paintings, about the studio she had back in Chicago, about the pieces that her parents hated and the ones that she loved anyway.

She laughs at her own jokes, and even in this form, I swear I can feel my chest expand just listening.

Freya paints the world around us with fresh eyes. She shows me colors I never knew existed until her light chased away the gray that distorted my view. Through Freya's eyes, the world is alive again. *I* am alive again.

When this war is over, and we are able to return home, I will find her every brush, every pigment, every scrap of canvas she could ever need. I will give her this world the way that she gives me life.

Vital. Flourishing. And in full color.

When the sun dips toward the horizon, we stop. We cannot risk a fire, still being too close to known rebel camps. But we should be safe enough to rest for the night. The others settle into a circle, quiet and alert. Freya sits beside me, picking at the food that I give her.

"You should eat," I say.

"So should you," she says, gagging as she sees Kiran eat a chunk of meat. "I don't think that I can stomach it," she adds quietly.

Internally berating myself for not considering her dietary preferences, I put all of my bread and cheese next to hers. "Take mine," I offer quietly.

"Caz—"

"No arguments."

She sighs and accepts it, but not without a mutter. "Losing a few pounds isn't going to hurt me."

The growl that leaves me is low and involuntary. "Do not say that."

She blinks. "It was a joke."

"You have no idea what I see when I look at you, do you?"

When she looks back down at her food, I grip her chin gently and force her to meet my gaze. "Strength. Fire. Beauty. You are perfect to me, Mo Sholas. Exactly as you are."

"You're going to make me cry again," she replies, voice shaky.

"Good," I say. "That means you believe me."

She nods before brushing her lips against my own in a kiss that is so gentle, it almost hurts. "Thank you for reminding me."

The others pretend not to listen, though Bran coughs pointedly and Gemma mutters something that sounds like, "Get a cave."

I grin. "Come on."

I lead her a little away from camp, to a small clearing where the moonlight spills silver across the grass. It is quiet here, just the wind and our breaths.

When she looks up at me, eyes bright and uncertain, I cup her face in my hands. "You do not ever have to doubt how I see you," I whisper.

And then I show her.

No words, no promises. Just the steady language of touch and trust. The world falls away until it's only us, heart to heart, as I worship her body in the moonlight.

# 16

## A Whole Ass Dragon

Freya

There are worse ways to wake up than cocooned in warmth and muscle. For one glorious, sleepy moment, I have no idea where I am. All I know is that something very large and very warm has wrapped around me like an oversize space heater with a pulse.

Then the heartbeat. Under my cheek and in my chest. Caz.

I groan softly, trying to stretch without waking him. His arm tightens automatically, dragging me back against him. Protective even in sleep. Typical.

"Good morning, sweetheart," he murmurs. "Go back to sleep."

I snort. "Your version of a pillow is way too solid. And I need to go find the little ladies' bush and pretend like you can't hear me pee."

"I did not hear any complaints about my tendency to be rock hard last night."

"Well, it does have certain advantages, I suppose."

His chuckle vibrates through me, deep and satisfying, and I seriously consider never moving again. The air is crisp, the light soft and gold, and I feel safe. Like the world outside this little circle of warmth doesn't exist.

Of course, that's when the shouting starts.

I sit up so fast I nearly smack into his chin. "Please tell me that's just Kiran arguing with Bran about breakfast again."

Caz's expression hardens instantly. Gone is the teasing warmth, the shift from lover to Chief happens in a blink. "Stay here," he says. "Do not move until I come back."

"Define 'stay here.'"

"It is exactly what it sounds like, Freya."

"Yeah, see…that's not really going to work for me."

He levels me with that look, the one that could probably make lesser mortals turn to stone. I fold my arms. "Don't even bother. You know I'm not letting you run off while I sit here like some useless damsel. I will worry too much at every sound, and I won't be able to handle it."

"Freya—"

"Nope. Save the speech, Chief. Let's go."

For a second, he looks torn between throttling me and kissing me senseless. Then he mutters a curse that sounds suspiciously affectionate and jerks his head toward the trees. "Fine. But you do exactly as I say."

"Wouldn't dream of doing otherwise," I say, and yes, I'm absolutely lying. There is no way that I am just sitting back while he charges into danger.

We move fast, crouched low, through the underbrush. The closer we get, the louder the chaos. Roars. Clashing. Snarls that make the air vibrate. My pulse spikes. Caz signals for silence and we crawl up a small ridge overlooking the clearing where the clan camped.

And there it is.

Our clan, surrounded. Outnumbered at least two to one. Massive shapes move below, bears in battle form, fur matted, teeth bared. The rebels.

"Could be worse," Caz whispers.

I glance at him incredulously. "Really? How?" The odds look pretty shitty to me.

"They could have brought twice as many."

"Comforting."

He scans the scene, every inch of him coiled, calculating. "We can win. My people are stronger, better trained. But we need a distraction to draw them off long enough for us to break the line."

I glance at the chaos below, then at him. A slow, dangerous little spark lights in my chest. "Distraction, huh?"

"Freya," he warns. "Whatever you are thinking—"

"—is probably brilliant," I finish for him. "Trust me?"

He exhales through his nose, clearly torn between Chief and whatever part of him actually enjoys my insanity. "You are not telling me what it is, are you?"

"Nope. Just in case it doesn't work. I need to prematurely save myself the embarrassment."

He stares at me for a long second. Then, with a groan, he kisses me and lifts me up into the tallest nearby tree. "From here, you can see everything," he says, steadying me as I climb. "You will be safe."

"Define 'safe.'"

"Do not fall. Do not get eaten. And do not die."

"Such high expectations. Really stellar pep talk, babe."

He smirks at my sass. "Whatever you are planning, make it big and make it fast. I will handle the rest."

"Deal," I whisper. And then he is gone, a blur of motion disappearing into the fray below.

My heart thunders. The sounds of battle rise and fall beneath me. Shouts, crashes, the roar of massive bodies colliding. My hands tremble, but not from fear. Focus. I can do this. I *have* to do this.

I close my eyes. Picture it. Something huge. Terrifying. Something no one here would dare fight. Not a bear. Not a wolf. Something that shouldn't even exist.

I don't know where the image comes from, maybe some childhood story or pure imagination, but *it's* vivid. Scales like molten gold, eyes like wildfire, wings cutting through the clouds. I can see it. I can almost *feel* the heat of its breath.

"Okay," I whisper to myself. "Please don't explode, brain."

Magic hums under my skin, stronger than ever before. It surges through me, wild and electric, as I shove it into the image, pouring every ounce of fear and will into shape.

For a heartbeat, nothing happens.

Then, the world shifts.

Wind whips through the trees, the sky darkens, and a sound tears through the morning. A roar so deep, it rattles my bones.

Below, the battle freezes.

I open my eyes just in time to see it. A massive, blazing shape sweeping across the sky. Shadow and flame rolling over the clearing.

A whole ass dragon.

Enormous and terrible and glorious.

The rebels scatter as panic spreads like wildfire.

"Holy fuck," I whisper. "It worked."

It's more beautiful than I imagined. More *alive*. I can feel it draining me, though. The energy bleeding fast, my fingers tingling, vision blurring. I grit my teeth. "Come on, hold. Just a little longer…"

Caz leads his clan, striking hard while the rebels are in chaos. The dragon flies overhead one last time, lets out another thunderous roar, and then bursts into golden light, dissolving like fireflies into the dawn.

I slump against the tree trunk, shaking. Exhausted. But alive.

Below, Caz looks up and finds me instantly despite the tree cover. He wears an expression of fierce pride, relief, and something achingly tender. It nearly undoes me.

I flash him a grin and mouth, *you're welcome.*

He shakes his head, smiling that dangerous, secret smile that means I'm absolutely in trouble later.

And honestly? I can't wait.

# 17

## Exceptions for Near-Corpses

Casimir

The roar fades, but the echo stays. Low. Vibrating through my bones, like the earth itself has not realized it is over.

The clearing is chaos. Smoke. Mud. The stench of blood and fear. Rebels scattering like frightened animals. My clan standing stunned, panting, bruised but alive. And above all that, the fading shimmer of gold light drifting down through the trees like embers.

Freya's embers.

Goddess, what did she just *do*?

I shove through the clearing, barking orders. "Check your wounds. Stay in pairs. Do not chase." They move automatically, their trust in me steady, but their eyes keep darting upward, where the illusion had vanished.

I don't blame them. I saw it too. The wings. The fire. The impossible.

The air is buzzing with magic. *Her* magic.

My chest is tight as I run towards the ridge. Freya is slumped against the trunk of the tree, pale and trembling. Her hair is tangled from the wind. Her eyes are half-shut. All of her remaining strength is put towards remaining nestled in the cradle of the branch. She looks small. Breakable. Absolutely infuriating.

"Freya," I bite out, pulling her gently from the tree.

Her eyes flutter open. "You're not dead," she croaks, and manages a shaky smile. "Good. I was worried that I hallucinated the whole thing."

I press a hand to her cheek, cool skin, damp with sweat. "What the fuck were you thinking?"

She blinks up at me, disoriented but still smirking. "You said you needed a distraction. You're welcome."

"A *distraction*, not...not..." I gesture helplessly at the sky, still glittering faintly with her leftover magic. "Whatever the fuck *that* was."

"That's a weird way to pronounce 'thank you.'" She snorts. "You have to admit, it was effective."

"Effective?" My voice cracks like a whip. "Freya, you just drained yourself nearly to collapse. You could have—" I stop, jaw clenching. I cannot even bring myself to finish that sentence.

Her eyes soften as if she hears the rest anyway. "But I didn't. I didn't fall, or get eaten, or die. Just like you instructed."

"But you could have," I snap. "You do not *ever* risk yourself like that again, do you understand me?"

Her head tilts, lips pulling up into a smirk. "Chief voice. Always so bossy."

"Freya."

She sighs, half-exasperated, half-affectionate. "You know, for a terrifying bear man, you're kind of adorable when you're panicking."

"I am not adorable. I am furious."

"You're scared," she says softly.

That stops me.

Because she is right.

"Of course I am scared," I grind out. "You think I can watch you burn yourself out and just, what? Smile and say thank you?"

She opens her mouth, but I lean in before she can speak, forehead resting against hers. My breath is still ragged. "Please do not put yourself at risk. I would not survive if you disappeared like that creature."

Her breath catches. "You wouldn't lose me that easily."

"Do not test it."

For a long, suspended moment, the world narrows to just us. Her heartbeat against my hand, the heat of her skin, the stubborn set of her jaw. She is too pale, too shaken, but she is alive. Thank the goddess, she is alive.

Then she smirks faintly. "So...was it at least a good dragon?"

I pull back just enough to glare at her. "*Good?*"

"Well, you're the resident expert on big scary things with claws."

I cannot help it, a short, incredulous laugh breaks out of me. "You are unbelievable."

"Thank you,"

I shake my head, still fighting a losing battle between worry and admiration. "If you ever scare me like that again—"

"You'll what?" she interrupts, eyes bright despite her exhaustion.

"I will find a way to tie you to me so you cannot nearly die pulling stunts like that."

Her smile turns slow and dangerous. "Promise?"

"Mo Sholas."

She laughs weakly and lets her head drop back against the tree. "You really need to work on your threats. They keep sounding like invitations."

I exhale sharply, dragging a hand over my face. She is impossible. Brave and reckless and so bright it hurts to look at her.

I glance back at the clearing. My clan is regrouping, the last of the rebels have retreated into the trees.

The fight is over. For now.

When I look at Freya again, her eyelids are drooping.

"Sweetheart," I murmur, softer now. "Stay with me."

"M'fine," she mumbles. "Just sleepy."

I slide an arm under her knees and another around her shoulders, lifting her easily. She mumbles something about 'bossy bears' and lets her head fall against my chest.

"Sleep," I whisper against her hair. "I have you."

As I carry her back toward the camp, the first rays of sun break over the treetops, gold light spilling across the bloodied field, warm and fragile. Renewed.

I look down at her, at the stubborn, brilliant female who just conjured a legend out of thin air.

If she is the fire, I will gladly burn.

The weight of her in my arms feels both too light and too heavy. She is incredible and I do not take for granted the trust that she places in me when she is most vulnerable.

By the time I reach the clearing, everyone has shifted back to their human forms, claws and fur giving way to skin and sweat. They look from me to the sky, where the last streaks of gold fade into ordinary sunlight.

Kiran is the first to speak. "Caz, what—what was that?" His voice wavers between awe and disbelief. "We've never seen anything like it."

"Neither have I," I admit. My tone is low, rough. I do not stop moving. I need to keep her close, feel the faint rise and fall of her chest. "It was Freya. She called it a dragon."

Gemma wipes a streak of blood from her cheek. "That was her doing? Do dragons live in her world?"

A ripple moves through them. Shock. Awe. Fear.

"She called it from nothing," I explain. "Held the illusion long enough to break the rebels' line, but she nearly burned herself out."

Bran mutters a curse. "Her Sun Kissed magic is *that* powerful?"

"I have not heard of Sun Kissed magic being that great," Kiran adds. "Your mother and sister possessed incredible magic. But this?"

I nod my head in agreement, unsure what else to say. Freya's magic is unmatched in comparison to the Sun Kissed blessings that I have been witness to.

Bears do not fear much. In our shifted forms, we are the largest species. Yet, I can smell the edge of it, wonder mixed with dread. A creature such as what she created belongs in myths, not in our world.

"We need to keep moving. The rebels will come back once they see that the dragon is no longer here."

Kiran shifts fully into his bear form, shaking out massive shoulders, and lowering—a silent offer to carry us.

I climb onto his back, careful to cradle Freya against my chest. She stirs once, mumbling something about 'giant lizards' then slips back into a deep sleep.

As we start down the valley, wind rushing over us, my mind replays what I saw. That roar. They way it seemed to crack the world open. The shimmer of scales, molten and impossible. The reflection of fire in its eyes.

I have fought battles. I have faced death. But nothing has ever stopped me cold the way that did.

It was not even the dragon that did it.

It was her.

Fragile, feisty, brilliant Freya, holding the sky and all those under it hostage with nothing but will.

Awe and terror twist together in my chest. If she can do that once, what happens next time? Where is the limit before the magic demands *her* as the price?

My instincts tell me to keep her in my arms. To hide away, let the world burn around us. But we need that power. The rebels will not stop. The war will not end because I am afraid of losing her.

So I start planning. She will have to practice—even more than we have practiced before. Smaller illusions, shorter bursts, until her strength builds like a muscle. I will be with her for every step, making sure that she learns control.

I will not let it eat her alive.

The sun dips low by the time I call for camp. We are deep in the forest again, hidden among violet leafed giants. We will need to risk a small fire, just one long enough to cook Freya's dinner. She needs more than bread and cheese to regain her strength.

I set Freya gently down on a bedroll. Her skin already has more color. Relief hits me so hard, it almost knocks the breath out of my chest.

I skewer the meat, coaxing the flames to a steady glow. The smell fills the clearing—smoke, salt, and a faint sweetness of sap as it sizzles in the flames.

When she finally stirs, it's slow and hazy. "Something smells good."

Her voice is scratchy, but her spark is back, rising to the surface where it belongs. She blinks up at me, hair wild, eyes bright. "Are you...cooking?"

I glance over my shoulder. "Miracles happen."

"Should I be worried?"

I huff a laugh. "Possibly."

Freya sits up carefully, wrapping the blanket tighter around her shoulders. "I thought it wasn't safe to have a fire."

"I make exceptions for near-corpses."

Her returning smile is sleepy but smug. "Flattery and grilled meat. You're spoiling me."

"Eat first," I say, handing her the plate. "Then you can insult my culinary skills."

She does not need convincing. Within minutes, she is devouring it like she has not eaten in days. Watching her eat, watching life come back into her cheeks, undoes something tight in me.

When she reaches for my plate too, I hand it over with a smirk.

After she is full, she sighs, tipping her head back to look at the stars through the trees. "That dragon looked so real. I know that it was just a magic trick, but it felt like it was real when I was pouring my magic into it. I almost fell out of the tree in shock."

I grunt. "It felt pretty fucking real from where I was standing too."

She nudges my leg with her foot. "Don't pretend you didn't love it."

"Love you nearly dying in front of me? Not quite."

"No," she says, eyes glinting. "The dragon. Admit it, it was impressive."

I huff a laugh, shaking my head. "It was terrifying."

"That was the point."

"I am not sure *that* much terror was necessary. That beast was the size of a mountain."

She leans back on her hands, smirking. "Fine. Next time, smaller terrifying creatures. Maybe something more manageable. Like…centipedes."

A shiver rolls through me. "Absolutely not."

She grins, unrepentant. "You're right. That is too terrifying. We need something that just looks scary but doesn't have a million little legs to skitter around on."

"Like you?"

Her laugh is quiet and breathless, curling warm in my chest. "Exactly like me."

The firelight dances over her face. Soft gold. Soft skin. Fierce eyes. I do not say what I am thinking; that no illusion she could ever make will match the awe of watching her stand against the dark.

She shifts closer, settling with her head against my shoulder, and I wrap an arm around her without thinking. Her hair smells like cherries, tinged with smoke from the fire. She smells like home.

"Caz?"

"Mm?"

"I know you're going to lecture me again tomorrow."

"You can count on it."

She smiles faintly. "But thank you for caring."

I press a kiss to her lips. "You never need to thank me for that."

The fire pops, scattering sparks into the dark. My clan settles nearby, low murmurs fading into the night. Freya nestles closer, whispering half asleep. "Next time, smaller dragons."

I smile into her hair, wrapping her tightly in my arms, and stay awake long after she drifts to sleep, watching the flames die down. The forest is still again. Safe, for now.

And in that quiet, one thought keeps circling back, steady as a heartbeat. If she is destined to be our dawn, I will eliminate any shadows that threaten to darken her light.

# 18

## Mini Monsters & Angelic Anal

Freya

There's something mildly humiliating about practicing illusions while riding a giant bear through the wilderness.

Kiran's fur is warm under my legs; the steady rhythm of his stride is almost hypnotic. The morning sun filters through the canopy, painting everything in a soft gold that I long to put on canvas. It should feel peaceful. It *would* feel peaceful, if I weren't trying to conjure miniature monsters in my hands like some traveling circus act.

The first attempt of the day fizzles instantly. A pulse of gold light, then nothing.

Caz's lips press against my neck. "That was a better start than yesterday."

"Yesterday, I barfed all over your feet," I remind him. "Better is simply keeping all of my insides on the inside."

"Progress is progress," he reminds me, flicking his tongue over my Mate mark.

I shift my legs closer together and bite back a moan. This is definitely not the time or place for the level of need he is stirring within me.

Kiran growls, making Caz chuckle against my shoulder.

"Easy for you to say. You don't have to concentrate while sitting side-saddle on a moving bear."

I know his mouth is twitching with a smirk even without looking back at him. "The only bear you will straddle is me. If that is how you prefer to ride, you are more than welcome to turn around and straddle my lap right now, Mo Sholas. Or my face. Whichever seat you would prefer."

I make a noise halfway between a snort and a groan. Between recovering from my magic use and sticking close to the clan for protection, we have not found many opportunities to be alone this last week. Clearly, Caz is feeling as needy as I am.

"For some reason, I don't think that will help me focus." I look down at my hands again. Gold sparks shimmer between my fingers, slippery as sand. The trick, apparently, is to focus without forcing. To invite the magic instead of wrestling it into shape.

That's my current theory, at least.

"Smaller," I mutter under my breath. "Think small. Harmless. Manageable."

The image forms before I can stop it. Tiny wings, bright eyes, mischievous grin. A miniature dragon no bigger than my palm, with its tail coiling lazily in the air.

"Holy shit," I gasp.

"Freya—"

"Don't you dare jinx it." I hold my breath as the little thing flits upward, wings beating fast like a hummingbird. It lets out a high, indignant chirp, then promptly dives nose-first into Caz's shoulder.

He flinches just enough to make me grin. "You're under attack, Chief. Take cover!"

Caz glances at the illusion as it gnaws on his arm. "She is adorable."

"Adorable is a form of fear," I argue, biting back a giggle. "Ask anyone who has been bitten by a puppy."

He laughs, low and rough.

"Next, I'm thinking…moderately menacing monkey? Ooh! Or a ravenous rabbit."

"Terrifying," he deadpans.

"Exactly," I smile. "Nobody would expect a rabbit to be their downfall."

He shakes his head, but there's a smile tugging at his mouth. "You are impossible."

"And yet, here you are. Riding with me on a bear like a loyal bodyguard-slash-audience to my magical genius."

"I like to think of myself as more of a safety supervisor, here to prevent your brain from exploding all over my cousin's back."

"Stop talking dirty to me, bear man. You should add that to the list of talents we were discussing earlier."

"And what would be on your list?"

"Sarcasm and chaos, obviously. Also, occasionally saving the world—though I guess that is more of a 'to do' list item."

"Feel free to add me to *that* list, sweetheart."

"You're already there, Chief. In permanent ink."

Caz slants his mouth over mine and kisses me until I'm breathless. A promise of fulfilling that particular mission once we bed down for the night.

The tiny dragon flickers with my distraction, its glow dimming. I catch it cupped between my hands before it can vanish entirely. "Easy," I whisper. "Stay with me." The magic hums, steady but fragile. My pulse quickens with it.

Caz's lips brush my ear. "Do not push it, Mo Sholas. Let it fade when it wants to."

I nod, loosening my grip. The little creature dissolves in a shimmer of light, leaving behind nothing but a warmth in my palms.

"Better," he says quietly. "You did not drain yourself this time."

"I also didn't save the day with a glorious sky dragon," I remind him. "So, mixed results."

He chuckles. "Glorious sky dragons are best reserved for emergencies."

"Define 'emergency.'"

"When my heart stops again because you have found yourself in danger…again."

"So…Wednesdays?"

"Freya."

"Fine, fine. Smaller monsters only. Maybe an insanely intimidating inchworm."

Caz exhales through his nose, clearly fighting a smile. "You are lucky you are good at this."

"Good? I just accidentally assaulted you with a sparkly lizard."

"It is still an improvement," he says, seriously. "And you did not faint."

"That is how you measure success?"

"For now, yes."

"I must be insanely impressive to you then. Think of all the times I could have passed out but didn't."

"The goal is to not pass out at all. Now be a good girl and keep practicing."

"Bossy," I mutter, though my heart is doing ridiculous things. He can feel it too. The quickening of my pulse. He pulls me closer, just enough so that I can feel his hard cock against my hip.

I lean into it as he drags his teeth along my jaw. "I am just using my skills to keep you motivated."

Despite the walking…erm…riding distraction that is my Mate, I focus my attention back to my hands, summoning another swirl of golden power. It flares, soft and steady this time. A glow, not a blaze. Contained. Controlled.

Small, but mine.

By the time we stop for the night, my mind is exhausted, but my body is on fire. Caz spent the entire day teasing me with his mouth, his words, and small touches that have me so worked up, a small gust of wind could probably tip me over the edge.

But now? Now, he has been moving about the camp, busying himself with anything other than me. And I know what he is doing. So I do it too. Is this a game that I want to play? Not really. Am I going to just roll over and let him win? Abso-fucking-lutely not. He might have the power to turn me into putty, but I refuse to cave first.

At this point, we have been dancing around each other for over an hour. The fire that was lit to cook dinner is burned down to a low glow, throwing lazy sparks into the night. The forest hums with quiet sounds.

And Caz? He is sitting across from me, pretending to sleep. The firelight licks over his skin, giving his dark skin a metallic glow, highlighting his muscles in a way that would melt my panties if I was wearing any.

"Stop staring," he murmurs, eyes closed.

I jump. "I wasn't." I totally was.

"You were." One corner of his mouth curves. "I could feel your eyes on me."

"I assure you, my eyes are still exactly where they belong." I toss a pine cone at him. He catches it effortlessly, sets it down, then looks at me with that quiet, devastating smile that makes my heart forget how to function.

Fortunately, my brain is still working, so I fight through it. He is waiting for me to break, to beg him for some relief from the pulsing need that has lived in my core for the entire day. But I am a strong, independent woman. And I don't need to beg a man to assist me. I can do it myself.

Quickly glancing around the camp, I see that the only set of eyes on me belong to my Mate. I lower my hand beneath the blanket that covers me, maintaining eye contact with Caz. I find myself dripping. *Needing.* Even the lightest brush against my clit sends a bolt of pleasure through my body. I can feel our shared heart rate accelerate, both from my arousal and his as he watches me dip a finger inside myself.

If looks could kill, his would burn me alive.

And I love it.

His jaw tenses and he inhales, swallowing down a groan that I know was about to break free.

"Come here, Freya."

"No thanks" I say breathlessly.

I hear Gemma snort a laugh, my cheeks heating when I realize that I am not being as covert as I originally thought. But also, fuck it.

I continue slowly finger fucking myself, taking more pleasure from having an audience than I would have suspected. I am about to add a second finger when Caz stands, abruptly, leaping over the dwindling fire, and throwing me over his shoulder. He runs, carrying me further into the forest, leaving the laughs at camp to float in the wind.

When we are far enough away from camp to have a bit of privacy, Caz sets me on my feet, spinning me around, and pressing my front up against a tree.

"Naughty," he growls in my ear, bringing my glistening fingers to his mouth. I press my ass into him, grinding against his hard cock.

"You started it."

"And soon, we will both finish. But first, a snack."

Caz drops to his knees behind me, spreading my feet wider apart and bending me at my waist before he flips my clothing out of the way. I am bared to him. His warm tongue licks me through my entire crease, first sucking on my clit and then swirling his tongue on my asshole before working his way back down to repeat the process.

"You are so wet, Mo Sholas. Did you enjoy having an audience back there?"

"Yes," I admit with a hiss, unable to lie. The proof is running down my legs.

Pressure builds higher and higher with every stroke of his tongue. Just when I am about to tip over the edge, he stands, chuckling against my shoulder as I whimper.

"Do not worry, sweetheart. We are only just beginning."

He lines the head of his cock up with my entrance, skewering me in one long, slow, stroke. Then, he spits. I can feel the warm liquid as it slides down my lower back and over my ass. Caz uses his thumb to collect the spit before gently pushing it into me.

He fucks me hard and steady, the bark from the tree scratching against my hands as I hold on. He adds another finger to my ass, fucking both holes in a punishing rhythm. His pierced head hits so deep inside me, I am sure it has left a mark.

"Come on my cock, Freya. Get it nice and wet, because I am taking your ass next."

"Oh, fuck," I shout as my orgasm blasts through me. He curses too, almost dropping me as my legs give out with the force of my orgasm. He lowers us both to our knees, before pressing his cum covered cock into my ass.

He goes slow, giving my body time to adjust around him. It hurts, the size of him being far too much for comfort. But I invite the burn. I know that once I have adjusted, he is going to make me feel so good.

"Breathe, love. Push back towards me."

I do as he says, relaxing my muscles and feeling instant relief once he is past that initial ring of muscle.

We both let out breaths as he gathers me closer, banding his arm around me so that I am leaning back against his chest. My body ignites everywhere that our skin touches, like tiny fireworks erupting just beneath the surface.

Unlike how he was fucking me earlier, Caz pumps into my slow and gentle, reaching down to rub my clit and relax me further.

"You are being such a good girl, Mo Sholas, taking my entire length into your tight ass. This was supposed to be a punishment but, goddess, I think this might be the afterlife."

My laugh is cut off by a moan that rips free when he increases his speed. "Did you just say that my ass is heaven?"

"If the goddess says it is my time, this is how I want to go."

His speed picks up again, the silent forest being filled with the sounds of flesh slapping flesh and our heavy breaths.

"You are so obsessed with me," I sass.

He laughs, loud and labored, as his hand cracks down onto my ass cheek, making me gasp and then moan as he rubs his hand over it to soften the sting.

"Tomorrow," he says into my ear, "I am going to fuck that mouth."

"Promises, promises," I pant, so close to orgasm that it is difficult to form words. He knows it too, because he spears three fingers into my pussy, fucking me hard and fast as I shatter into stardust. The force of my orgasm obliterates me and spins me into an endless sea of bliss.

Caz comes too. There is a part of me that feels his cock thicken impossibly and then shoot jet after jet of cum deep inside me. But it is like I am experiencing it all from afar. Like I am in an entirely different universe, the string connecting our hearts being the only thing stopping me from floating away.

I am in a daze as he carries me to the river's edge and gently cleans us up. I am in a daze as we return to camp, not at all caring about the looks and comments that we receive from the clan. I am in a daze as he snuggles me up with a blanket, holding me closely to his body.

In that moment, the world could have been ending, and I would not have noticed. Because all that mattered—all that matters—is him.

When I wake, it's to the sound of breathing that isn't quite right. I can feel our shared heartbeat pick up, begin to race, as I am held firmly to Caz's side.

The fire has burned down to ash and the forest is heavy with the kind of silence that means *something is coming.*

Noticing that I am awake, Caz's arm squeezes just a little tighter. His muscles are coiled with tension. Something is wrong.

Kiran's shadow moves at the edge of the trees. Everyone in the camp is awake but pretending not to be. There are no words being exchanged, just the subtle, deliberate stillness of trained warriors holding their breath.

I stay still, my cheek still pressed against Caz's chest, eyes mostly closed, as the air tightens around us.

Rebels.

They must have followed our trail. Probably convinced that the dragon was a trick of the light, or maybe they are just betting that we have used up all of our luck.

Caz shifts just enough to whisper, his lips brushing my hair.

"Stay still. They have us surrounded."

I murmur back, so low it's almost a breath. "Define 'surrounded.'"

"At least a dozen. Maybe two. They are waiting for a signal."

"Good. So are we."

He tenses slightly, like he can already hear the reckless idea forming in my head. "Freya—"

"Shh." I don't move, but my pulse quickens. "I've got it."

He doesn't argue, which is both a surprise and a warning. He knows he can't stop me once I decide.

I close my eyes again, reaching for that spark under my skin. The hum of magic that always feels a little like holding sun rays in my palm.

I picture it first. Always start with a picture.

Big. Crawling. Fanged.

Hundreds of them.

A grin twitches at the corner of my mouth. "Let's give them nightmares."

Caz exhales sharply. "What are you doing?"

"Taking inspiration from classic childhood trauma."

And then I let it loose.

The magic blooms, thick and hot, crawling up my chest like static. The air goes cold for half of a heartbeat, and then the forest moves.

From the trees above, they drop.

Massive, glistening, eight-legged nightmares. Webs shimmer silver in the moonlight, and hundreds of smaller ones pour down the trucks, legs clicking softly.

I know it's not real. I *know*. But when one skitters across my arm, even I have to fight back a scream.

Kiran mutters something unholy under his breath. Gemma swats at her shoulder. And still, every one of us stays still, playing along. Waiting.

Then the rebels break cover.

A dozen shapes creeping closer—until the first one spots the nearest spider.

The scream that follows, high pitched and terrified, as a massive man jumps and turns to run away, will live rent free in my head for the rest of my life. I didn't know it was possible for someone so big and burly to make *that* noise.

I bite my lip, shaking with suppressed laughter as chaos explodes. Roars, shouts, the cracking of bones and branches as enormous bears shift mid-run to escape the crawling wave of horror.

My spiders, hundreds of them now, chase after the fleeing rebels, climbing, leaping, webbing everything in sight. The air is filled with the sound of absolute panic.

Within minutes, they're gone. Nothing left but the trampled undergrowth, a few stray webs, and our entire camp stifling hysterical laughter.

I didn't even break a sweat.

Gemma's doubled over. Kiran's wheezing. Even Bran has tears streaming down his face.

I let the illusion fade with a sigh, the last spider dissolving into rays of sunlight.

Caz's arm tightens around me as he finally lets himself laugh too.

"You," he manages, his voice rough with amusement, "are terrifying."

"Thank you," I say primly. "I do my best."

He shakes his head, still smiling. "I have fought battles, faced monsters…and yet nothing will ever compare to the sight of warriors paralyzed because of your imaginary spiders."

"You said I should go smaller next time."

"Smaller, yes," he says, eyes bright. "But somehow so much worse."

He tilts my chin up, expression softening in that way that undoes me every single time. "You are incredible, Freya. Reckless, brilliant, impossible. And so far beyond anything I ever imagined."

My chest goes tight. "You're just saying that because I saved your furry butt. Again."

"No," he says quietly. "I am saying it because every time I think I have seen the limits of what you can do, you tear the sky open a little wider."

Heat floods my face. I look away, mumbling, "You should probably work on being less poetic."

"And you," he murmurs, brushing a stray hair from my cheek, "should work on accepting a compliment. Because I will never stop telling you how amazing you are."

We stay locked in that moment, a foggy haze of love and desire swirling between our shared breaths. Then, Gemma pops our bubble by shouting, "Next time, maybe conjure something *cute*, Freya!"

I groan despite the smile on my face. "Like what? A litter of kittens?"

The whole camp dissolves into laughter again, Kiran and Bran swapping ideas back and forth on the most terrifyingly cute creatures I could create next.

Caz doesn't laugh this time. He just watches me, smiling like the world has gone mad and he's fine with it.

And in that look, under the thinning moonlight, I realize something terrifyingly simple. If he ever stops looking at me like that, I think I might shatter into dust—just like my illusions.

# 19

## Try



Two days since the spider illusion, and I can still hear the laughter echoing in my head. It was the first time in years my people laughed like that. Without fear. Without burden. And it was the first time I let myself truly believe that maybe, just maybe, we could have a future filled with more moments of joy.

Now, that hope feels fragile again.

The wind whispers of trouble, and I know that we will soon be swarmed with the responsibility of fulfilling this prophecy.

We are close to Claw Keep. Close enough that every familiar scent pulls up memories I have not touched in years. The trees here are different from the ones near Paw Keep. They are thicker, older, their roots winding through the forest like veins. And somewhere within them, invisible until you are nearly upon it, lies the keep—a fortress disguised in the wilderness.

Freya shifts on my back, the weight of her small body a steady warmth against my spine. She has been quiet for hours, head resting just behind my shoulders, her fingers absently brushing though the fur at my neck. She thinks the tremor of fatigue goes unnoticed, but I feel it. I feel it in the way her hands tentatively glide over my fur, in the way her breathing is punctuated with heavy yawns, in the slight change to her heartbeat that pounds in my chest.

Even with practice, every time she uses her power, it costs her.

I promised myself that I would never let her feel the strain of burnout.

But I also know that promise will break the moment she needs to save someone.

We move in silence until I signal the clan to halt. The keep lies somewhere beyond the next ridge. It is close enough that I can almost taste the old stone on the wind. I lower myself to the ground so Freya can slide off. She stretches, rubbing sleep from her eyes, then leans against my leg, her body fitting at my side like it was made to.

"Whose idea was it to get such an early start? If you want me to maintain my youthful good looks, I am going to need more beauty rest, Chief," she murmurs, still half asleep.

I huff out a soft, rumbling sound that makes her smile. Bears do not laugh, not properly, but she always seems to know when I am trying.

Kiran moves ahead to scout, melting into shadow between the trees. The rest of us stay low, quiet, hidden in a thicket of dark, towering giants.

And while we wait, I think.

I always think too much when I am in this form. When I cannot speak, when all I can do is *feel*. The memories come easier in bear form, maybe because instinct does not lie.

I grew up here. Running through these woods with Cal and Sol, pretending we were kings of the forest. Sons of blessed bloodlines. The elders used to call us the "Three Suns"—among the next generation meant to guide the clans into peace. To protect the females of our lines. Built bigger, stronger. We thought that meant we were invincible.

Now, only the three of us remain. Our families, our legacies, gone to ash and story.

And still, our names echo in the prophecy.

*There will be Three Sons of the First.*

*Claw, Paw, and Maw.*

Sometimes I wonder why I was left standing when so many stronger and more important fell. Why was I spared the attack that took my mother, my father, and my sister?

Now, I understand.

I was meant to survive because *she* was meant to live. Because Freya is more important. And I am meant to protect her. To make sure that her light—terrifying, brilliant, and untamed—never goes out.

She shifts again, sighing softly. I glance down at her and cannot help but think—when this is over, when we survive, maybe I can have what I always wanted.

A home that is not haunted by ghosts.

A family.

Her laughter echoing through the quiet halls instead of battle soaked forests.

Children, maybe. Cubs with her bright light.

If that is something she wants too.

If fate does not demand more from us than it has already taken.

A sharp crack of a branch snaps the daydream in half.

Kiran.

He bursts through the undergrowth, shifting mid-stride, landing hard in human form. His face is worried. His chest heaving.

"Caz," he says, breath ragged. "It's bad."

The clan gathers quickly. Freya straightens beside me, already alert, reaching for my hand now that I have shifted back into skin.

Kiran does not waste time. "There is a battle—just over the ridge. Claw is under siege. Callum and his Mate are the only ones still standing."

My stomach drops. "How many?"

"Dozens. More than we have ever encountered. They are in the clearing near the keep. Callum is swarmed. He is holding his position, but barely. His mate—goddess, Caz, I've never seen anything like it."

He looks at Freya as if the words themselves aren't enough. "She is like you," he tells her. "But instead of illusions, she radiates sunlight. She wields it like a force. I watched her throw bears five times her size with a single blast."

Freya's eyes widen. "Like a bomb?"

Kiran shrugs. "Whatever it is, it's draining her fast. They will not last much longer."

The silence that follows is heavy and certain.

Freya's gaze turns toward the ridge, jaw tightening. "Then we must move fast."

I know that look. It is the same one she had before she made a dragon out of thin air.

"Freya," I start, turning to meet her gaze. But she is already moving. Pacing. Her expression is calm in that terrifying way that always means she is about to do something impossible.

"I have a plan," she says.

My heart sinks. "Of course you do."

She glances at me then, eyes fierce, alive with that strange light that makes everyone else step back and me step closer. "But it's going to take more power than I've ever used before."

"Then we will find another way," I say, tucking a wild lock behind her ear.

Her hand finds mine, steady and warm. "No. We don't have time for another way. Cal and his Mate are fighting for their lives right now. If we wait, they die. And if they die, so does the prophecy."

I grip her hand tighter. "*You* are not expendable."

"Neither is *she*," she offers me a soft, brave smile. "We do not know what is going to happen if we try. But we know exactly what will happen if we don't. We *have* to try, Caz."

And goddess help me, because even knowing how much it might cost her, I already know that I will be by her side, watching her shine.

# 20

## *Willa*



Caz looks over at me. His eyes asking the question that we both already know the answer to. *You are going to do something reckless again, aren't you?*

And he's right.

"I have a plan," I say aloud, mostly for the others. My voice is steadier than I feel. "It's risky, and I'll need to use more power than I ever have before to hold it."

Kiran huffs. "You aren't about to summon another dragon, are you?"

I almost laugh. "Not this time."

The entire clan stares at me expectantly, only Kiran and Caz in their human forms. But I can see the support in Gemma's eyes. I can see the smirk on Bran's face. This is my clan now too, and they are willing to follow along with whatever I have planned.

"I'm going to make them think that we have an army behind us. Hundreds of bears, charging the field. Enough to send the rebels running before they realize that we are actually the ones who are outnumbered."

Kiran blinks. "You can do that?"

"She can do anything," Caz says at the same time as I say, "I hope so."

I can feel Caz's worry as it radiates off of him and yet, he stands next to me as a pillar of support. I wrap my arms around him, pressing my body firmly against his and dragging his mouth to mine. "I will be careful," I say against his lips. He exhales before bruising my lips with the force of his kiss.

Leaving me breathless, he pulls back and tips his forehead to mine, staring so intently, I feel it in my soul. We don't need more words. I know what he is saying without them. *I hate this, but I trust you.*

Shifting, he lowers himself back to the ground, allowing me to climb up onto his back. Another silent promise. *Whatever happens, we do this together.*

I can feel it before I see it. The air buzzes with magic, like a static charge that feels as if it is calling to mine, bringing the light in my veins closer to the surface.

When we crest the ridge, my breath catches.

The forest ahead is chaos—trees splintered, the ground torn up by careless paws as they charged through the treeline. Just past the trees, in the center of the clearing, a huge bear with chocolate brown fur and violet eyes matching my Mate's. And on his back—

"Willa?" The name slips from my lips before I can stop it.

For a heartbeat, I think I'm imagining her. My brain trying to fill in something I miss so desperately it hurts. But no—she's *there*. Standing barefoot on the bear's back, sending pulses of sunlight out from her body.

Willa. My best friend. My sister in every way but blood. The girl I thought died the same night I did.

I bite hard on the inside of my cheek to stop the sob clawing its way up. Not now. Not here.

Later, when we're both still alive.

Right now, she's fighting for her life—and I am going to do everything that I can to help her.

Okay. Focus. Numbers, not details. This is what I have been practicing for. The dragon was one big image—a mountain of flame. The spiders were hundreds of smaller, simple shapes. This...this will need to be both.

I glance back at my clan, focusing on the three bears directly behind us. Kiran, Gemma, and Bran. All in their bear forms. Massive, powerful, familiar. Perfect templates. I let my gaze move over each of them, memorizing the angles of their shoulders, the gleam of their fur, the glint of teeth in the morning sunlight.

Then, I close my eyes and copy.

Not one.

Not three.

Dozens. Then hundreds.

Each shape ripples out from me like echoes in a mirror, slightly different each time. I shift fur color and vary size, but one by one, each bear comes to life, taking form in such a real way, I have to remind myself that they are just illusions. Tricks of the light.

The strain hits instantly. It's like fire behind my eyes, blazing through my veins. But the image holds.

I open my eyes to a sea of beasts, stretching behind us.

An army that doesn't exist.

And I pray to any god that might be listening, to please let this be enough.

"Ready?" I whisper, my voice raw.

Caz dips his massive head once, muscles coiling like springs beneath his fur.

"Now!" I command, the world exploding into motion as my clan and my illusion run as one giant force, tearing down the ridge and straight into battle.

Caz's roar shatters the air, a sound so deep and thunderous it vibrates through my chest.

My own voice joins in his roar, yelling for someone who I never thought I would see again. "Willa!"

The rebels freeze. Then scream.

Chaos. Glorious, terrified chaos.

I hold my illusion, gritting my teeth as the army behind us drains my power. But I don't take my eyes off of Willa. I can't. She continues sending out blasts of power, but I can tell that her magic is draining too. I can *feel* it as if it is connected to mine.

Confusion and disbelief flicker over her face as she takes me in. I'm sure it is quite the sight to see, charging into battle on the back of a massive bear, leading an army of *other* bears into battle.

None of this seems real. And yet, it has never felt more right.

By the time we reach the center of the clearing, the rebels are shocked still or retreating back into the trees. We slow to a stop near the brown bear who must be Callum, and I slide off Caz's back. My knees nearly buckle under the strain of the illusion, but adrenaline keeps me upright.

Willa pulls a similar maneuver and runs straight for me.

"Holy hell," I whisper, and then we crash together— arms around each other, tears mixing with blood and mud, falling to the ground in a pile of laughter that sounds too wild to be sane.

"You're alive," she says over and over, running her hands over my face as if she thinks that I am just an illusion. "I thought I lost you."

"Right back at you, babe," I rasp, pressing my forehead to hers. "You didn't think I would let you fight alone, did you? Let's end this."

Then we turn, hand in hand, toward the battlefield.

As soon as our palms meet—light and illusion works as one. Together, we unleash everything we've got left. Golden flares blast from her chest while my phantoms charge around the last rebels, hemming them in until there is nowhere left to run.

Beside us, Caz and Callum roar.

And as the final echo fades, I glance at Willa. She grins at me, wild and tear streaked.

"I knew the universe wouldn't get rid of you that easily."

"Please," I say, breathless but laughing. "It's going to take more than death, rebellion, and inter-dimensional chaos to stop me."

She squeezes my hand, her smile trembling at the edges. "Don't you dare disappear again."

"Not planning on it."

Because now, I have too much to live for.

# 21

## *Rut Fueled Fuck Fest*

## Casimir

The room Callum gave us smells of cedar and rain. The kind of scent that seeps into your bones and tells you that, for tonight, you are safe. We are in the same wing that my family always stayed in when we traveled here. I was afraid that it would stir up ghosts, but with Freya by my side, there is no dark to let them in.

Steam curls upward in slow threads of mist as we soak in the tub. Freya sits with her back to my chest, my arms circling her, her damp hair clinging to her flushed skin as it glows in the soft firelight.

I trail a hand along her thigh, half a caress, half an anchor, letting me know that this is real. She is here. She is safe.

"I still can't believe she is alive," she whispers softly, smiling. "I keep waiting for the universe to pull another cruel trick, but no. That's Willa. Loud, stubborn, Willa."

"You grew up together?"

"Since we were little girls," she nods. "My parents weren't always awful. When I was young, they loved me. Maybe they still did when I died. But it was more obvious back then. I had a heart condition. A hole that I was born with. I almost died, my lips turned blue, and they brought me to the emergency room. I had surgery to repair it. Afterwards, the doctors suggested my family join a support group with other families who went through similar things. That's where I met Willa and Sloane. Our lives took different paths, but we always carved out a place for each other."

"And then you came here."

She meets my gaze, unreadable for a moment, then nods. "Maybe fate just has a weird sense of humor."

I brush a wet strand of hair from her cheek. "Or maybe it knows exactly what it is doing. Maybe you were drawn together in your world because you were both meant to be here, in ours."

Freya leans back, dropping her head to rest on my shoulder. "When Willa and I were fighting today, when our magic overlapped, it was strange. I could *feel* her power. Not just see it or sense it. It was like we were pulling from the same current. The more we worked together, the stronger it got."

I still. "You shared power?"

"I think so." Her brow furrows against my jaw. "It wasn't like draining or giving. More like...blending. Like two streams meeting."

My gut twists, equal parts awe and unease. "If that is true, then together, the two of you could move mountains."

She looks up at me, giving me a dry look. "Let's start with not collapsing after five minutes of magic first."

"Modest goals," I say, lips quirking.

She flicks a droplet of water at me. "Realistic goals."

I chuckle, but my thoughts are already turning darker. *What if it is not just blending? What if one current pulls harder than the other.*

I shake away those thoughts. Willa loves her. I have to believe that their magic is a blessing.

Freya nudges me. "Hey. You're thinking too hard again."

"Guilty," I admit. "I just...please promise me that you will be careful."

"Careful is my middle name," she deadpans.

I raise a brow. "Liar."

She laughs. "Fine. But I promise, Caz. We will be careful. Willa won't hurt me. Not even accidentally."

I want to believe her. I *do*. So I nod, and let the worry slide somewhere quieter in my chest.

After a moment, she sighs, resting her head on her arm along the tub's edge. "You know what I keep wondering?"

"What?"

"If Sol's got one too. A magical human, I mean. You said the three of you—Callum, Sol, you—were the last Sun Kissed bloodlines, right?"

"Yes." I reach for the soap, tracing lazy circles along her shoulder as I speak. "We grew up together. We were brothers in all but blood, like you and Willa. When the old world fell, I thought the gods were cruel to spare me. But now I see the pattern. Maybe we were meant to survive because *you* were meant to come."

She looks up at me through the rising steam, eyes darker than the bathwater. "That's a lot of faith to put in fate."

"It is not fate I trust," I say softly. "It's you."

For once, she doesn't have a quip ready. She just watches me, quiet, the firelight reflected in her eyes like stars sinking into amber.

The water starts to cool, but the air between us warms with every breath. Her fingers find mine under the surface, gliding up my wrist, over my chest.

"Caz," she murmurs, and there is nothing teasing in it now. Just want. Just trust.

I rise, water streaming off my skin, and pull her with me. She gasps as I lift her from the tub, her legs wrapping instinctively around my waist.

"Always carrying me around," she mutters against my neck, voice thick with amusement and heat.

"I like reminding you that you're mine to protect," I growl back.

She tilts her head, lips brushing my jaw. "Protect, huh? That's what we're calling it now?"

"Call it what you will, Freya." I lower my forehead to hers. "You are my miracle. My fire. My chaos. And I will spend the rest of my life trying to deserve you."

"You already do," she says firmly as her fingers clutch at my shoulders, trembling—not from fear, never from fear— and something inside me splinters with the weight of it. The sound of the fire is distant now, softened by the pulse in my ears. Every place our skin touches feels alive, burning with the quiet rhythm of her breath against mine.

"Tell me what you need, Mo Sholas." I bury my face in her neck, smiling as she raises her hips in search of mine. "Everything that I am is yours."

"Show me," she says, dragging her teeth against my Mate mark. "Show me how much you love me with your hands and your mouth and your cock. I already feel you in my heart. I want to feel you in every piece of me."

The way her eyes find me… it's as if I am something worth believing in. And I can't fathom it. How I, made of mistakes and ruin, could ever deserve the kind of grace that looks at me the way she does.

When my mouth finds her skin, it isn't hunger that drives me, not really. It's worship. The taste of her is sweet nectar on my tongue, the kind of holiness I used to think the gods had forgotten. My thoughts blur with each slow touch, each sigh that trembles from her lips.

How did I ever become this lucky? To be paired with her, bound to her, chosen by whatever strange and patient fate wove her life into mine? I will never be enough for her light. But I will spend eternity trying.

She moves beneath me, whispering my name, and the sound threads through me like a vow. I think of all the things I am not—whole, worthy—and then I think of her, and it doesn't matter. Because she is everything I could ever wish for.

I feel her heartbeat beneath my palm, steady and wild, and I know—whatever the cost, I will not give her back.

Settling my head between her thighs, I run my nose through her center. This is how I want to start and end every single day. Freya's fingers twist into my short hair, holding me firmly to her pussy as I lick firm swipes from ass to clit.

She moans, rocking herself against my face as she demands more of the pleasure I am offering.

Holding her thighs open, I devour her, not coming up for air until she is screaming my name and soaking my face. "Good girl," I praise, nipping at her over-sensitized clit before flipping her onto her stomach and pulling her ass into the air. I shove blankets and pillows under her stomach for support before I dive back in, giving her ass the same attention I just gave her dripping cunt.

"Fuck, Caz," she moans, pushing herself back towards me. I can feel her body tensing as she approaches another climax, but she shocks me completely by pulling away from me right before she gets there.

"I need you in my mouth," she explains, pushing me onto my back and positioning herself over top of me with her pussy back in my face but where she can suck my cock into her mouth.

"You want me to spill down your throat?"

She moans, sending an amazing vibration straight to my balls. "Yes. I want you to claim me everywhere. My mouth, my pussy, and my ass. Fill me with your cum, Chief. I want you dripping out of my pores. I *need* it."

"Fuck!" I roar, shooting jets of cum into her mouth.

Before she has had time to swallow, I flip us around and ram my cock into her pussy. She screams at the intrusion, but through our heart bond, I can feel that it is from pleasure and not pain. She wants me unleashed.

I fuck her so hard, I can feel the wooden supports on the bed cracking. She comes alive beneath me, clawing and moaning as her wet heat sucks me in deeper.

"More, Caz," she begs. "Give me it all."

The bed collapses under us, but I don't stop. I *can't* stop. I am so lost in rut, the only thing that could pull me out of this lust fueled haze is Freya. And it is clear in her eyes that she has no intention of stopping.

She spasms and screams, her body giving in to the release that had been building, and pulls me over the edge with her.

"Tell me to stop," I plead through gritted teeth as I pick her up and push her against the wall, her legs wrapping around me as if that is exactly how they belong. "I can't be gentle, sweetheart. Tell me to stop."

Freya looks up at me with lust filled eyes, pupils blown, and I know she is seeing the madness that I am lost in reflected right back at me. I can't stop, but I take a moment to recognize the heat that is radiating off of her. Fuck.

"Callum!" I roar as loud as I can, my bear providing extra power despite the primal haze he is locked in.

Moments later, Cal and Willa burst through the door, immediately taking note of the broken bed and our current position as I try to keep Freya's body covered with my own.

"Um..." Willa says, shocked because to her, it would look like I just called them in to witness me fucking her friend.

A low growl rumbles in my chest, my bear feeling threatened by having others in the room while we are vulnerable. "Rut," I force out. "Heat."

"What is rut?" Willa asks. "Freya's in heat?"

I continue thrusting in and out of Freya as she moans and writhes in my arms. "Can't...stop."

Willa comes closer, stepping to stand next to Freya despite Cal trying to keep her behind him. Fur sprouts from my arms and I force my hold on Freya to loosen so that my claws do not puncture her delicate skin.

"More, Caz. I need more," Freya whines, begging me to sate the heat that is burning in her veins, clawing at my shoulders.

"Tell...me...to...stop," I tell Cal, needing him to help me protect my Mate.

"Casimir, stop!" Cal commands, putting as much dominance in his words that it should have caused us to snap out of it. But it doesn't. My bear is too far gone, too dominant to let another bear tell him what to do.

The only real relief that I can feel is that I know that Freya is not hurt. For now, she is just feeling the intense need that is brought on from the heat. I would never intentionally hurt her, but a couple in rut and heat can be a very dangerous thing. I could never forgive myself if my bear pushes her too far.

Then it happens. A bright light disrupts my vision, blasting me down and away from my Mate. My bear growls again, but the force was enough to let me regain control of my body.

Freya is now in the arms of her friend, who must have caught her, stopping her from crashing onto the floor. But Willa's magic did nothing to cool Freya's need. She cries, trying to scramble closer to me, fighting with her friend as she tries to hold her back.

"It's okay," I tell them all calmly, breathless. "I'm okay now. My rut must have triggered a heat for her. She needs my cum."

Willa's face flames red as she looks to Cal, who is smirking at her reaction.

"You have control?" he asks me.

"Yes." I nod.

"We will wait outside until we know for sure that you will not slip back into rut."

"Thank you."

As soon as Willa releases Freya, she is in my lap, spearing herself onto my cock. "I need you, Caz. Fill me."

"I know, Mo Sholas. I am here now. I will make you feel better."

# 22

## Honey?



The first thing I notice is the cold.

The second is that the bed is gone. Or, more accurately, dead. Splintered posts. Torn bedding. A massacre of wood and fabric.

I'm lying on a pile of blankets on the floor, wrapped up like someone has attempted to make me into a burrito. My whole body feels like it has been stretched, wrung out, and set on fire.

Embers glow in the hearth, glowing faintly in the gray light leaking through the window. My head swims.

"Chief?" My voice cracks, sounding small.

The door opens so fast, it bangs against the wall. He's there in two strides, barefoot and half dressed with wild eyes. Then everything in him softens at once, like he has been holding his breath for hours.

176

"Mo Sholas," he breathes, dropping to his knees beside me. "Goddess, you are awake."

"Barely," I smirk, trying to sit up and immediately regretting it. My limbs feel like overcooked noodles. "Did I run a marathon or something? Why does everything hurt? And why am I on the floor?"

His face goes still, and the muscles in his jaw shift as if he's choosing every word with care. "You do not remember?"

I shake my head slowly. "The last thing I recall is you…uh…" My cheeks heat. "You eating me out like I was your last meal. Then, nothing."

He lets out a shaky breath and sinks back on his heels, scrubbing a hand over his face. "Freya, I am so fucking sorry."

"Okay, you saying that in that tone is not comforting," I say, crossing my arms the best I can. "What happened to the bed?"

His mouth twitches, but there is no humor in it. "That was me. Or rather, my bear."

"Your bear broke the bed?"

He nods grimly. "Freya," he says, voice soft but strained. "My bear went into rut. It hit suddenly. I did not have time to get control before it…before *he* took over. It was still my body, but when rut happens, instinct takes over. It made me stronger. Wilder. Not myself."

"Oh." I stare at him for a beat. "Like a heat?"

He runs a trembling hand through his hair, and I can see the guilt in every line of him. "It triggered something in you, too. Like a heat. Your body was reacting. I couldn't trust myself not to hurt you. I didn't have any control. So I called for help. Callum and Willa came. They helped break me from my rut and then stayed close until you were satisfied enough to fall asleep."

I blink. "So, you're telling me that my best friend and her Heart Mate, who I just met for the first time yesterday, saw all of...that?"

He winces. "I swear I tried to keep you covered—"

I laugh. "Oh, I'm sure you did. And Willa is never going to let me live this down."

"I am so sorry," he says again, quieter this time. "If I could have stopped it on my own, I would have. I did not mean to put you in a position that—"

"Caz." I reach out, catching his wrist. His pulse thunders under my thumb and in my chest. "Look at me."

He does, reluctantly.

"You didn't hurt me. You didn't even *try* to hurt me. You recognized what was happening and you called for help. That is not a weakness. That is power. You kept me safe."

His brow furrows. "It didn't feel like power."

"Maybe not," I say, gentler now. "But you made the right call. That's what matters."

He studies me, like he's afraid I'll change my mind if he blinks. "You're not afraid of me?"

I let out a soft laugh. "Caz, I've watched you turn into a bear the size of a small house. I think I can handle a bout of extreme horniness."

His lips twitch, but his eyes stay troubled. "If you need space to process this, I understand. Truly. I would not blame you."

"Stop saying that." I shift closer, pressing a hand to his chest. His heart beats fast beneath my palm. "You did everything right. I mean, yes, it's *mortifying* that Willa and Callum saw me like that, but I'm not angry. It just feels a bit weird to not remember."

"I am not sure you want to remember."

I tilt my head. "That bad?"

His mouth softens. "You were perfect. But neither of us were at our best. They saw me fuck you against the wall, sweetheart."

The sincerity in his voice squeezes my heart. "Well, hopefully they at least got my good side."

He laughs quietly, finally relaxing. "You are impossible."

"Resilient," I correct. "And apparently durable, judging by how much of me still functions."

That earns me a small smile. "Are you hurt anywhere?"

"Just sore," I admit. "Every muscle feels like it ran a marathon without asking me first. But I'm fine."

"Truly?"

"Truly," I say. And then softer, "You kept me safe, Caz. Even when you couldn't control the bear. That's what I'll remember."

He exhales, shoulders sagging like a weight's been lifted. "I was so scared," he confesses, voice barely a whisper. "I could feel it happening, but I could not stop it. It was like watching it all from above. I could see it and feel it, but I was not really there. I couldn't reach you. Keep you safe."

I touch his cheek, thumb tracing the line of his jaw. "But you did reach me. You did keep me safe. You always do."

Something fragile and bright flickers in his expression. His hand covers mine, holding it there.

"Goddess. What did I ever do to deserve you?"

I smile faintly. "Probably saved a small village or something in a past life. Or maybe you just got lucky."

He huffs a quiet laugh, forehead dropping to mine. "Lucky," he repeats.

We stay like that for a while, the air thick with exhaustion and relief. When he finally stands and helps me to my feet, I wobble but don't fall.

He grins down at me. "Radiant."

"Radiant is one word," I mutter. "Disheveled swamp nymph might be another."

"Beautiful," he says simply.

"Flatterer."

We move through the morning routine slowly—him fussing, me rolling my eyes. My body aches, but it's the kind of ache that promises recovery, not harm. Like I worked out more than I ever have before. Which is probably accurate.

As I dress, my mind wanders ahead to the next inevitable challenge. Ugh. I will need to face Willa and Callum. I might combust on sight. But at least I wouldn't be around any more to feel the embarrassment of having to look them in the eye and pretend like they didn't see my vagina swallow Caz's massive dick.

I sigh. "Do you think I should bring them something? A peace offering?"

He arches a brow. "Like what?"

"I don't know. What's the bear shifter equivalent of a fruit basket? A jar of honey? A bottle of whiskey? A plaque that says *Thanks for being the magical cock block that we needed to stop the lust crazed fuck fest that was going down in your guest room. PS. Sorry for showing you my coochie and breaking the bed?*

Caz laughs, full and warm. "I think they will just be happy that you are okay. And clothed."

"Maybe," I say, sliding my hand into his as we head for the door. "But I'm still buying honey."

Making a quick stop at the kitchen, we walk hand in hand into the dining room, our arrival causing several sets of eyes to glance our way. Supplying the entire room with the joy of receiving an awkward little wave, I let Caz lead me further into the room before sitting down next to Callum and Willa, pulling me onto his lap.

"I can sit in my own seat, you know," I protest.

"Yes. I do know that you are capable of sitting without me, Mo Sholas. But my bear is riding me a bit hard after last night and this was the compromise that I made with him."

"What was he pushing for?"

"He wanted me to spread you out on this table and feast between your thighs so that all of these unfamiliar bears know who you belong to."

I gulp, my face flaming red. "Oh."

Willa giggles at the exchange from her perch on Callum's lap. Remembering our last interaction, or not at all remembering but being informed after the fact, I turn to our hosts and offer a sheepish smile. "Honey?" I offer, holding up the jar.

Callum looks over my shoulder to Caz, who nods, before accepting the jar from me.

Not saying anything in return, I feel compelled to explain. "I felt like I needed to give you some kind of apology for everything that you witnessed last night but what do you get someone who, despite just meeting them, has seen your pussy? I mean, that is just the truth of it. Anyway, I wanted to get you something to say sorry and I thought that maybe honey would be the right call but now that I'm thinking about it, do bears even *love* honey or is that just something that was made up from our world? Either way, I had my heart set on honey being the best peace offering but then Caz reminded me that there isn't a friendly neighborhood grocery store in this world so I snuck into the kitchen and stole the honey to bring to you. It's the thought that counts, right? Also, if the stolen honey is decent enough currency, is it possible to get a new, not broken bed?"

The entire room is silent for a beat before erupting in laughter. After the room calms down, Willa wipes the tears from her eyes. "Fuck, I missed you."

# 23

## Fang Fetish

Freya

I'm sweating.

Not the cute, glowy "oh look at me, I'm a magical chosen-one girl boss" type of sweat.

No.

I'm talking, armpits of betrayal.

Which is rude, because the morning breeze is crisp and cool across the training clearing. Trees tower overhead, golden beams of sunlight spearing through the branches like spotlights auditioning for a divine interrogation scene. The Mother is humming under my feet with slow, patient energy—like she's watching, judging, and politely asking me not to face-plant.

"Okay," Willa says, planting her fists on her hips. "Show me your illusion."

"The one where I pretend last night never happened?"

Willa snorts. "Babe, there was nothing fake about what I saw going down...or, in, I guess."

I cover my face dramatically. "When did my life become such a tragedy?"

"An adventure.," she counters.

"Complete and utter fiasco."

"At least it comes with a gigantic side of pierced dick," she says brightly.

"There is that," I conceded as we eye fuck our men, shirtless and sparring. We are supposed to be practicing our magic. And we *are.* But who wouldn't be distracted with literal sex on legs grunting and glistening just a few feet away? "Do you think we can get them to take off their pants too? With the proper motivation, I might not feel so inclined to illusion myself six feet under."

"They are definitely more like seven feet, but I will gladly go under that hunk of man meat any day of the week. No illusion needed."

Mid-spar, Callum laughs, clearly having caught more of our conversation than I had intended.

Caz smacks him playfully. "Don't encourage her," he says. But when my eyes slowly pan up his body, he's grinning at me like I'm his whole world. Our joined hearts stutter. Fuck, he's gorgeous.

Willa leans closer and stage whispers, "For the record, you handled the surprise mini-heat beautifully."

"Gross. Also, beautifully? I have zero memory of what happened—"

"Ouch, Mo Sholas. You are doing great things for my ego," Caz jokes.

"But," I continue, "I have been told that I climbed him like a tree and then clawed at you like a rabid raccoon when you wouldn't let me at him."

She snorts. "True, but he was still into it, and that is all that really matters. He looked like he was about to combust on the spot. Honestly, you're welcome. We saved your Mate from spontaneously exploding."

Cal chuckles. "I would bet all my gold that he exploded. Multiple times, I would imagine."

Caz drags a hand down his face. "Can we not—"

Stepping closer to Caz, I pat his arm. "Baby, if we don't make fun of it, the awkward wins. Do you want the awkward to win?"

He exhales, defeated. "Not particularly."

"Good." I stretch up on my tip toes and place a kiss on his jaw, before turning around, setting my stance, and wiggling my fingers. It has zero effect on my magic wielding, but it seems important in movies, so I figure it doesn't hurt to add it in. "Okay. Illusion practice. Round three. Let's see if I can make something besides an accidental giant squirrel this time."

"Hey, don't discount the usefulness of a giant squirrel. It chased Cal for twenty minutes," Willa reminds me cheerfully.

"It had fangs," Callum mutters. "Real ones. You gave it real fangs."

"I'm going to be *real* honest with you here, Cal—can I call you Cal? You have seen my vagina so I think we have probably skipped over a few of the early steps of friendship and are firmly in shortened name territory. Anyway, Cal. I am sorry that my pretend squirrel scared you. But I didn't mean to give it fangs. I panicked. And if I have learned anything about myself through this entire process, it is that *everything* gets teeth when I panic. Luckily for us, there is a good chance that I will also panic when we are saving the world, so it will probably work to our advantage."

"Now that you mention it, I think everything you have created has had fangs," Caz adds.

"Fang fetish?" Willa asks, waggling her eyebrows at me.

I snort. But, maybe?

"There was the dragon," Caz continues. "Then the small dragon that chewed on my arm. That one definitely had fangs. Then there were the giant spiders—"

"Aragog?" Willa asks.

"Obviously," I admit.

"The bear army did not have fangs, but there were plenty of sharp teeth involved." Caz laughs. "Maybe you do have a fang fetish. We can explore that later."

He steps behind me, sliding his hands to my hips to adjust them. "Your stance needs grounding," he murmurs, voice low and smooth in that way that sends a bolt of heat straight to my clit. "You keep leaning forward."

"That's because my center of gravity is permanently off due to emotional trauma and my love of cheese."

His fingers tighten. "I like your center of gravity exactly where it is."

"And I like you pretending my stance needs to be adjusted just so that you have an excuse to feel me up when we are in public. We both know that I can cast in any position."

Willa fake gags. "Please. My ears. They're innocent!"

Cal wraps an arm around her waist and whispers something that makes her knees buckle.

"Okay," she says, a bit breathless. "My ears are less innocent now."

I bite back a laugh. The four of us make a strangely cohesive team. The Sun Kissed girls and our ridiculous bear shifter Mates. Who knew we'd survive being magically yeeted from our world into this one? Who knew we would end up as prophesied magic-wielders with the fate of the land resting on our messy, sarcastic, sun-burnt shoulders?

Not me, that's for sure.

I inhale, gathering the warm, humming energy inside me. It's like sunlight filtered through honey. Bright and thick and a little unwieldy. It pools behind my ribs, asking to be shaped. I picture the image clearly. Something simple this time. A wolf. No, a bird. Okay, a small bird. Like Flit from Pocahontas. Preferably without fangs.

The energy spills outward, flickering into form in front of us.

A bird...ish...thing appears. Willa and I both tilt our heads to the side as we process what we are seeing. It has wings. And eyes. Three of them. Oops. And when its beak opens...goddammit. It has teeth.

I groan. "Why teeth?! WHY?!"

Willa wheezes with laughter. "It's adorable in a nightmare sort of way. Like those ugly-cute purse dogs rich people carry around."

"I just don't understand how I can create a literal dragon one day and now I can't even get a hummingbird right," I whine.

Caz turns my chin to face him. "You used an incredible amount of magic when you created that army. Then, your body was thrown into a heat. Your well of magic is not at its strongest right now. That is okay." He kisses my lips. "Try again. Same animal, but go slower. Don't *push* the magic out, just let it flow on its own."

"I don't mean to rush it. The magic is just...eager."

"Like you were last night?" Willa chirps.

"Do you want to die?" I ask sweetly.

She beams. "Not this week. We still have to save the world."

Cal nudges her. "Be nice."

"I am nice," she says. "I'm a fucking delight."

"You are both of those things. But you are also a brat," he tells her with a smirk. "And you know what brats get?"

"Orgasms?" Willa and I reply at the same time, batting our eyelashes.

Caz presses his hard-on against my ass. "Hurry up and make a regular bird so that Willa can blast something and I can take you inside to break another bed," he growls into my ear.

I bite my lip. "You got it, Chief."

Focusing, I take another deep breath. This time, I take my time creating the image in my head, focusing on all of the details that I want to create. Instead of pushing the magic out, I focus on creating a door and then opening it, allowing the magic to pass through when it wants to. The magic curves, gathers, and—A perfect, golden hummingbird appears, flitting around like a Golden Snitch. No teeth. No extra eyeballs. No nightmares.

Willa gasps. "Fuck, yeah, Freya!"

Cal whistles. "That is impressive."

Caz presses a kiss to the top of my head. "I knew you could do it."

"The dragon was still cooler."

He snorts. "It also almost killed you." Lifting his finger into the air, the golden hummingbird perches. "I will take a thousand of these little beauties over one really cool dragon any day."

Warmth floods my chest. Pride, happiness, maybe a pinch of something terrifyingly close to hope.

Willa claps. "My turn! Let's see if I can do this without accidentally nuking us."

She steps forward, cracks her neck like action heroes do in movies, and squares her shoulders. Light gathers under her skin—bright and sharp. It is different from my honey-warm glow, but I can feel the pull of it in the air. Her magic builds, pulsing, begging to burst outward.

"Small," she whispers. "Controlled. Not a sun-grenade."

The beam shoots from her chest, thin and focused, as it hits the target Callum set up for her, throwing it back about 50 feet from where it stood.

She gasps. "I did it!"

I cheer. "Hell yes!"

Callum sweeps her into his arms. "That's my girl."

Willa wiggles her eyebrows at me over his shoulder. "Look at us. Competent."

I place a hand to my chest dramatically. "A true miracle."

The prophecy has been weighing on me. On all of us, really. It clearly calls out clans Claw, Paw, and Maw. That, combined with our magic—none of us asked for this.

But right now? Laughing with my best friend, our Mates teasing us, the two of us learning to control the Sun Kissed magic flowing through our veins…it feels possible.

Hard. Terrifying. Destined in a way I'm still not sure I deserve.

But possible.

Willa elbows me. "We're going to save this world, you know."

I smirk. "Oh, absolutely. And, we're going to look hot doing it."

I raise my hand, letting a small illusion spark in my palm—just a tiny, glittering, golden butterfly with itty bitty fangs.

"For The Mother," I say softly.

"And The Sun," she adds.

Caz and Cal join us, forming a messy, warm, slightly sweaty circle in the clearing. Whatever comes next, we will face it together.

Even if my magic comes with a bite.

Hey. We can't all be perfect.

# 24

## Chutes & Ladders

Casimir

The council room of the Claw Keep hums with tension. Golden streams of light shine through the glass, warming the stone walls and highlighting scars from the rebel attack that took far too many lives a few years ago. Out of the corner of my eye, I catch sight of the little illusions Freya is practicing while whispering with Willa.

"I forgot to tell you," Willa whispers to Freya, "I have a suggested upgrade you might be interested in."

"For what?" Freya asks.

"Well, I couldn't help but notice that your Mate's junk isn't as bedazzled as Cal's is."

Freya sputters, spraying droplets of her drink all over the table, drawing the attention of the entire room. "Sorry," she says with a cough. "Wrong pipe."

"All I'm saying is that there is something that could be added to make the right pipe even better." Willa leans in closer, actually whispering into Freya's ear, making it impossible for me to eavesdrop.

Whatever she says, Freya's cheeks flame red.

"What are you ladies whispering about?" Cal asks, amusement lacing his tone despite being interrupted.

"Decorations," Willa replies, batting her eyelashes.

"What type of decorations?" he asks, smirking like he already knows but wants her to say it out loud.

"Nothing for you to worry about, babe," Willa brushes him off. "We are talking about Caz's setup."

*My setup?*

Tor chokes. Colt looks skyward in silent prayer. Gemma leans forward like she's about to take notes.

Freya covers her face. "Willa, I love you, but why do you know what my Mate's setup looks like?"

Willa shrugs, entirely unbothered. "Because he was naked and feral and you were naked and feral and somebody had to dump a magical bucket of cock block on everyone. It was a mess, Freya. A beautiful, sweaty mess. But someone had to take one for the team and take note of all of the appendages."

Cal smirks. "Yes, love, you were very brave."

"Anyway," Willa continues, clapping her hands and refocusing with inappropriate enthusiasm, "the point is, Caz is missing the best ones."

"As you have just pointed out, you have seen his dong. If he adds anything else, there is no way it is going to fit inside me," Freya whisper-shouts.

"Trust me, babe. You will love it. It rubs the whole—"

Cal gently covers her mouth with his hand while I wonder how our war council took such a drastic turn into open discussions about my cock.

"Willa," Cal says, "We do not need to give details."

She licks his palm.

He yanks his hand back. Colt doubles over in laughter.

"Hypothetically, if we could still make it fit...what would you suggest?" Freya asks Willa.

Willa whispers the location into her ear.

Freya's eyes widen. "That's actually a thing?"

"It's a glorious thing."

She thinks for a moment, then flicks her gaze to me with an assessing, speculative expression that makes me nervous. "I can't believe I've been living without this knowledge."

"Right?" Willa claps again. "Girl, you deserve the full experience."

"Is anyone going to fill me in?" I ask.

Freya pats my cheek. "Nothing you need to worry about until later, Chief. Besides, the point is that *I* will be filled. Not the other way around. Though I wouldn't be opposed…"

"Later?" I repeat, alarmed.

Willa beams like a menace. "Don't worry, Caz. We'll have Cal talk to you."

Cal blanches. "I—what—no. Absolutely not."

Willa kisses his jaw. "You love me."

"Yes," he says immediately. "But no."

Freya and Willa exchange a look of shared, wicked purpose. I do not like that look. Not at all.

Cal clearly does not like it either. "We are in a strategic meeting about war," he reminds our Mates.

"Right, right," Willa says. "War now, Freya's chute and Caz's proposed ladder later."

Cal jumps right back into his discussion with our joint clans. I do my best to concentrate. I really do. But I cannot help my unwavering focus on my Mate. I would be lying if I said that my hunger for her was sated. Every inch of her is temptation and I need another hit of her sweetness like I need air to breathe.

Freya's thigh brushes mine under the table, steadying and undoing me in the same heartbeat. Her presence sparks heat in my blood and makes focusing during this meeting very difficult. Considering recent events, Callum clearly senses it too.

He does not even bother hiding his look of warning. "Casimir, if the two of you break another bed in this keep, I'm putting you on grunt duty like a cub." I snort a laugh. This might be his keep, but we both know he has no authority over me.

Freya leans forward sweetly. "Callum, dearest, you say that like you have no idea what demands the Mate bond makes, yet you would sprint across a battlefield if Willa so much as sneezed."

The effect is immediate. Cal's stern facade melts into open devotion as he looks toward his Mate. "A sneeze can be dangerous. If she is unwell, she will need me."

Willa, who is currently perched sideways in her chair with her feet tucked under her, snorts. "I literally blew a hole in your training wall last night."

"Yes," Cal says adoringly. "With breathtaking power."

She blinks at him. "I destroyed a load-bearing timber, Stud."

"And you were magnificent, Mo Chridhe."

Tor snorts. Colt coughs to hide a laugh. Gemma looks personally offended that a male can adore someone that loudly.

Freya leans toward Willa, stage-whispering, "I'm getting total golden retriever vibes."

Willa pats Cal's cheek. "My very large, very murdery retriever. But also, he likes to tie me up and spank me while he worships my pussy. Best of both worlds."

"Get it girl," Freya giggles.

Cal nuzzles her hand before remembering he is, in fact, the Chief of Claw and therefore has to have some dignity. He fails.

I clear my throat and force my attention to the map spread across the table. Three red stones mark reported rebel activity. Each has crept closer to the keep.

Closer to us.

Closer to Freya.

A hot coil of dread tightens in my chest.

Cal regains his composure—somewhat—and taps the map. "Three separate sightings converging within a week is no coincidence. The rebels are gathering here. They are staying about a day's run from the keep."

Tor folds his arms. "They are preparing for something significant."

"War," I say. "Or a decisive strike they think will end the clans once and for all."

Gemma nods grimly. "After five years of picking at the pieces of what they destroyed, they are ready to finish the job."

Freya's hand slips onto my knee under the table—warm, reassuring. My heart steadies. My bear presses up in a low, possessive growl I have to swallow down.

She is everything I cannot afford to lose.

Everything the rebels would destroy if given the chance.

"I won't let them," she whispers, just loud enough for me to hear.

My voice comes out rougher than intended. "You will not face this alone. I will stand at your side until my last breath."

She beams at me, like a sun rising just for my eyes. My pulse stumbles and she brings her hand up to her chest. A clear sign that she felt it too. Pulling Freya onto my lap, I catch her gasp with my mouth, needing to feel the press of her lips against mine.

Cal clears his throat pointedly. "If you two start fucking and break this table, I am going to make you sleep outside."

Freya breaks the kiss, blushing as she buries her face in my neck. "There are plenty of things for us to break outside too," I tell him.

"Focus, or we will be here all night," Cal scolds.

Willa pats his arm. "Let them be cute, Stud."

He turns to her. "They can be cute after this meeting, love. We need to stay focused."

I drag my teeth over Freya's Mate mark, making her squirm, before setting her back in her own seat.

Cal gestures at the red stones again. "The rebels want the scrolls destroyed, but we do not know if they know of the prophecy."

I nod. "They do not know where the scrolls are, either. My keep is well guarded, both by the land and the traps that we set. But it is possible that they have heard of the prophecy—just like how Tor knew about it through stories passed down."

"It has been passed down in my family since the beginning. But I did not know it was a prophecy until recently," Tor explains.

"If they do know about it, and they want it stopped, they will target us first. Claw, Paw, and Maw are named within the rhyme."

"That leaves Sol," Kiran adds.

"Have we heard anything from him?" Willa asks Cal.

He shakes his head. "It is not uncommon for him to leave messages unanswered. But, given the prophecy and the threat, it is unlikely that he will ignore my request for aid."

Freya props her chin in her hand. "So, do we think Sol has a human Heart Mate too? Another Sun Kissed human who was magically transported to this world?"

"Oh, he'd better," Willa says. "For symmetry. And drama."

"What magic would she have?" Freya muses. "Fire? Solar storms?"

Willa snaps her fingers. "Teleportation. To escape awkward small talk."

Gemma snorts. "Very useful."

Freya brightens. "Or maybe she can just make people spontaneously tell the truth."

Willa gasps, bringing her hand to her mouth. "Freya. What if she's nice?"

They exchange a look of mutual horror before doubling over in laughter.

I refocus them. "We need a strategy. If the rebels amass their army, they could strike the keep before we have any chance of reinforcements arriving."

Cal nods. "We will strengthen defenses immediately. I want extra patrols in the northern pass. Tor, Colt, you will run them. Make sure everyone has time to sleep between shifts. We will need to rotate everyone who is able."

They nod.

"Kiran," I say, "work with the scouts. Keep everyone moving. No predictable patterns. We cannot afford to lose anyone."

"Understood."

Cal turns to Willa, his voice shifts lower— commanding, but tender. "Love, you are training with me today. We need to be sure your blasts are directed and controlled."

She salutes. "Yes, sir."

Cal rumbles a pleased growl, and I know that they will not get nearly enough training done.

I face Freya, wanting nothing more than to throw her over my shoulder and bring her back to our rooms. Unfortunately, I need her to focus, and I am her biggest distraction. "Mo Sholas, you will train with Gemma while I help relay instructions to the clans. Small illusions."

She visibly prepares to argue, shoulders back, chin lifted.

I lower my voice. "Please, sweetheart."

The resistance melts. "Fine. Small illusions with Gemma. But you will need to make it up to me later. And I get to make whatever small illusions I want."

"You may," Gemma says, "but they cannot have fangs."

Freya sighs dramatically. "That's not fair. A lot of things naturally come with fangs."

"Not frogs," Kiran says under his breath.

"That was one time!" Freya exclaims.

"One time too many," Kiran says, rubbing the back of his neck. "They chased me."

"They were enthusiastic," she mutters. "It isn't my fault that they were so drawn to you. You just have one of those faces."

"Huh," Willa says, "he really does."

"What does that mean?" he asks, a look of horror and confusion on his face.

Ignoring the conversation that has completely gone astray, again, Cal rolls up the map. "We fortify. We prepare. And if the rebels come for us, they break on our walls. Colt, will you tell Mira that she needs to stay within the walls or shall I?"

Mira is a bear and panther hybrid who grew up with her grandparents in Cal's clan. She has a small cottage not far from the keep. From what I remember, Colt and Mira have a complicated relationship.

Colt mutters under his breath, letting Cal know that he will talk to her.

As chairs scrape back, Freya rises and threads her fingers through mine. My chest expands at the simple touch. She tilts her head. "Do you think we have time to break another bed before we need to act like adults with responsibilities?"

I chuckle, taking her mouth with my own. "Be a good girl and practice your magic. I will help you break another bed as a reward."

"Just let me know if you need another one moved into your room," Willa tells Freya with a wink. Cal lifts her effortlessly into his arms, causing her to yelp, laugh, and kiss him. He lights up like she put the sun directly into his life.

Freya snickers. "He's so gone."

"Hopeless," I agree.

# 25

## Committing to the Bit

Freya

Gemma says the training courtyard is "peaceful," which is a generous interpretation of a space where I have accidentally created—so far—one carnivorous frog, two bloodthirsty bunnies, and a very cute fox that somehow had the teeth of a shark.

In my defense, art school did not prepare me for magical creature conjuring. Unless you count that one professor who always called my work "aggressively whimsical."

Anyway, I'm standing here with sweat on my brow, my palms glowing warm and faintly gold, while Gemma pinches the bridge of her nose like she's reconsidering all of her life choices.

"Again," she says.

"You said that like twenty times," I whine.

"And I will say it twenty more if necessary. Your illusions need to reflect your intention. Not chaos."

"They can be both," I mutter. Obviously, it would be great if my illusions would come out exactly as I intended, but what I really need to focus on is holding larger illusions without burning myself out. We aren't going to win this war with hideously cute little animals.

Knowing what I am thinking, she levels a glare at me that could peel bark off of a tree. "Freya, if you cannot hold a small illusion, you will not be able to weaponize any illusions in the stress of battle."

"I feel like that's a rule you're inventing just for me."

She sighs. "Focus. Create the fox. No fangs. No horns. No surprising anatomical additions."

"That was one time," I protest.

"Maybe for the fox," she agrees. "But the sparrow had tusks. It couldn't even take flight under the weight of its teeth."

"It was avant-garde!"

"It attacked Kiran despite having to drag its face across the ground."

"It was committing to the bit. And you can't tell me that it wasn't terrifying. I bet it would have sent some of the rebels running."

Gemma groans skyward like she's begging The Sun for patience. I take a breath and lift my hands again.

Okay. Focus. Intention. What did my professors always say? *Draw what you see, not what you assume.*

Fine. I picture a fox. Not a vampire fox. Not a demon fox. Just a fox. Orange fur, bright eyes, fluffy tail. Zero interest in eating Kiran.

Warm light blooms between my palms. Shapes knit together. Fur, color, little ears, and teeth. Normal teeth.

I almost collapse with relief.

Gemma circles the illusion critically. The little fox wiggles its butt and sticks its tongue out at her. Apparently, some of my attitude bled into the design. My heart makes a soft, ridiculous bloom of pride.

Gemma grunts. "Acceptable."

"That's the highest praise you have ever given me."

"It is the highest praise you have ever earned."

"Clearly you are forgetting about the massive dragon I created to save your ass, but whatever." I smile. "Admit it. You're impressed."

"I am relieved," she says flatly. "Which is as close as you are getting."

I let the fox dissolve, magic dissipating like sparkling dust into the air.

Another breath. Another try. A butterfly—delicate, blue. No fangs. A small bird—feathered, sweet, not homicidal.

Gemma actually nods. Twice.

I preen like she handed me a gold star and a cookie. "So," I say, "does this mean my fanged-bunny phase is over?"

"Unlikely," she says, walking away. "But perhaps you will only terrorize our allies once a week instead of daily."

"Progress!"

Her voice drifts behind her and I can swear I hear a note of pride. "Meet your Mate. You are finished for today."

By the time I return to our room in the keep, I'm glowing with a mix of triumph, magic, and the deeply satisfying knowledge that I didn't create a single creature with an unapproved number of fangs in the last half hour.

I push open the heavy wooden door and stop.

A brand-new bed dominates the space.

It is massive. Reinforced. I swear there are metal brackets that weren't there before. The frame looks like it could survive a tornado.

Caz is sprawled across it like he was born there. Long and powerful and somehow both wild and romantic at the same time. He props himself up on his elbows when he sees me.

"Mo Sholas," he rumbles. The low timber of his voice sends a bolt of heat straight to my core. "You return victorious. I can feel your pride through our bond."

I smile, then gesture at the bed. "Did they build that thing for us or for the structural integrity of the keep?"

"For us," he says without shame. "Callum made several remarks about our previous enthusiasm."

I snort. "They aren't wrong. I plan to be very enthusiastic with you, Chief."

He pats the mattress next to him and I climb on, sinking into the soft furs. The bed doesn't even creak. Impressive.

Caz brushes a loose lock of hair behind my ear. "Tell me about your training."

I tell him everything. My disastrous first attempts. My artistic epiphany. Gemma's slowly deteriorating patience. He listens with the sort of attentiveness that makes me warm from the inside out. Other than Willa and Sloane, I have never had someone care about me like this.

He threads our fingers together. "You shape the world as easily as breathing," he says softly. "You are incredible, sweetheart."

The compliment lands directly in my chest.

I lean into him. "How was your day?"

"Patrols are set. Scouts move without pattern. The clans prepare." His tone shifts, becoming heavier but then he looks at me again and warmth returns. "And Cal asked that we refrain from breaking any more furniture."

"Asked politely?"

"Threatened colorfully."

I grin. That seems like exactly the kind of challenge we will happily push the limits of.

"So…did you have a nice chat with Callum this afternoon?"

"Mo Sholas," he says, voice dropping into that low, sinfully lyrical register.

"What?" I ask innocently, batting my eyelashes.

He snorts. "Do you have questions for me? You know that I will tell you anything."

"Well, I didn't have any questions until Willa brought up some possible additions to what you already have going on," I admit. "Are the piercings a Chief thing? I just thought that it was a bedroom optimization thing."

Caz throws his head back and lets loose a laugh. "That is an added bonus."

"Is it a tradition? Not everyone has them."

"Have you been looking at others, my love?"

"Market research. Not important. What's the deal?"

He shifts, sitting closer, his knee brushing mine. "When a female of the Sun Kissed lines is born, she is marked on her fifth birthday." He trails his fingers lightly over my golden Sun Kissed mark. "Males of those lines do not receive the same blessing. So, when we come of age, we undergo a ceremony. A piercing of gold. To signify that we may carry the line forward. That we are also chosen by the Sun to further the line."

I can't stop my hand as it reaches down to touch his piercings and smirk when a pleased growl rumbles in his chest.

"And only Sun Kissed are allowed to wear gold?"

He nods. "It is sacred. Our Goddess's metal. To steal it, as the rebels have done, is not only theft—it is blasphemy." His jaw tightens. "They have no respect for tradition. No reverence for the light."

I rest my hand on his thigh, squeezing gently. "I'm sorry."

His face softens instantly, covering my hand with his large one. "You bring light back to all we lost, Freya. I would give it all up again if it means meeting you."

My heart does a flip. A full gymnastic, stick-the-landing flip.

"If it is to show your status as being Sun Kissed, why is it not in a more visible location?"

His eyes darken in a way that sends a band of heat straight through my core. He leans close, lips brushing my ear. "What better place than where pleasure concentrates and magnifies? A golden point to ensure that every coupling between a male and his Mate is...magical."

Oh.

Caz inhales, groaning when he scents my arousal, pulling me to lay underneath his body, as he places kisses over my heated skin.

"Now tell me, Mo Sholas, which piercings you would like me to add."

All thought leaves my brain as he lifts my dress over my head and wraps his lips around my peaked nipple.

I try to answer, but all that comes out is a garbled moan.

Caz chuckles. "Tell me Mo Sholas."

"I think I might need a refresher on what you are already working with," I say as I guide the head of his pierced cock to my entrance.

"Whatever my Mate wants, she gets," he says as he thrusts into me in one hard motion, both of us moaning loudly once he is fully seated.

His hand slides to my hip, lifting my leg up so that he can press in further. My body melts into him, pulling more of his weight on top of me so that I can no longer tell where I end and he begins.

His mouth finds mine—slow at first, savoring. Then deeper. Hungrier. My fingers curl against his chest, feeling our shared heartbeat as it vibrates through me.

His thrusts increase, the sounds of our ragged breaths and the slide of wet skin fill the room. We lose ourselves in the moment—firm, delicious, building heat. His hands guide my body against his, drawing soft sounds from my throat that he quickly swallows. I drag my nails through his hair, earning a low groan that I feel everywhere.

Caz's lips trail down my neck, lingering at my Mate mark. My head falls back, breath shuddering.

"Caz," I gasp.

"I know, love." His voice is rough now, frayed with need.

I rock my hips up to meet him, increasing intensity as we both chase our release.

A knock slams into the moment.

"Dinner!" Willa shouts through the door. "Stop defiling furniture and get out here."

I bury my face in Caz's shoulder. "I despise her."

"Eyes on me, Freya." Caz continues fucking me—harder, faster—until I am no longer in control.

A second knock.

"She can hear us," I whisper-yell, still lost in pleasure and not stopping despite my growing embarrassment.

"Let go for me, love. Come all over my cock. You are already squeezing me so tight."

Bringing his mouth back to my neck, he bites down on my Mate mark, pushing me over the edge so forcefully, I scream my release."

"Fuck!" Caz roars as he thickens and shoots jets of cum so deep inside me, I can almost taste it.

"Well, I definitely heard *that*," Willa says from the other side of the closed door.

Caz presses one last kiss to my mouth—slow, deep, claiming—before sliding my dress back over my head and finding a pair of pants for himself.

I try to stand, but I haven't regained control over my limbs yet and I stumble on my way to the bathroom.

"Where do you think you are going, Mo Sholas?" Caz asks as he bands his arm around my waist and holds me against his body.

"To clean up for dinner?"

"Not tonight, love." He looks down at me with fiery heat still in his eyes. "Tonight you will wear my cum to dinner and then I will clean you up for dessert."

I open and close my mouth several times, trying to form a response.

"Try and keep in as much as you can," he adds, spanking my ass on his way to the door.

Willing my feet to move, I quickly run to catch up to him before he opens the door.

"But they will all know!"

His eyes burn with promise as a devious smile spreads across his face. Dropping his voice low, he brings his lips to my ear. "Let me know if you need my fingers to push my seed back into your pretty pussy at dinner."

A small moan slips out of my mouth as he reaches down to show me exactly how that will work.

Bringing his wet fingers to my mouth, he paints my lips and then lowers himself to take me in a bruising kiss.

"Let's go to dinner, love. We do not want to be late."

Opening the door, he grabs my hand and pulls me past a smirking Willa and Callum, who had definitely just listened to that entire exchange.

Peering around us, they look into our room.

"Ha!" Willa exclaims. "Their bed is still intact. You owe me an orgasm, Stud."

"You bet on us?" I ask, my entire body flushing. "What would he have won if we did break it?"

She snickers. "My ass."

"So, a win either way," I smirk.

"Exactly," she nods.

"The night is still young," I add, winking back at our guys.

"Oh, I'm counting on it."

# 26

## Early Morning Edging

Casimir

It has been a week since we first fortified Cal's keep. A week spent practicing magic and encouraging my Mate to keep trying. A week spent waiting. And waiting, I am learning, is its own kind of battle.

We gather in the war room just after dawn. Cal, Tor, Kiran, Colt, Gemma, and Mira all sit scattered throughout the room. The long table is crowded with maps, charcoal-marked trails, and the newest sketches of our fortifications. The keep groans around us, the bones of the old fortress strengthened with new barricades, sharpened logs, hidden traps that Colt swears will turn any rebel bastards into skewers.

Cal stands with his arms folded across his chest, the morning sun cutting a harsh line along his jaw. "They have stalled their retreat and are now three days out," he says. "Maybe four if the storm holds."

Tor snorts. "They are cowards. They saw Freya's illusion and ran."

"Not cowards," I counter. "Strategists. If they believed hundreds of bears were here, they would wait for reinforcements before losing more men."

Cal nods grimly. "Which means they will hit harder when they do come. They thought that we were nearly wiped out. They were not expecting a real fight when they attacked."

My hands rest on the table, palms flat, grounding myself in wood and purpose. "We need confirmation on where they are regrouping."

Kiran points at the map. "The last sign of movement was by the river pass. Tracks. Ash. Not fresh, but not cold."

"And Sol?" Tor asks.

Silence hangs like frost.

I exhale slowly. "Nothing."

Cal swipes his hand down his face. "He is stubborn, but he is not negligent. Something is keeping him from responding."

I do not say what we are all beginning to fear—that the rebel force attacked Sol's keep already. That they have cut communication, leaving the third Sun Kissed clan Chief lost to us.

The prophecy names all three of us. What will happen if we are not able to fulfill its demands? Prophecies are cruel things. They do not promise ease. Only necessity.

"Panthers?" Cal asks, shifting the conversation.

We all glance at Mira. Half-panther, half-bear, she wears both sides with quiet pride, though she hides the weight of belonging to two worlds behind snarky commentary and her need for independence.

She drums her fingers on the table. "You can ask," she says carefully. "But do not expect a reply. If the battle is not to be waged in their land, they will not believe it to be worth the risk."

"Our territory is not far from their borders. Surely, they would not stand idly by as we fight for the survival of our clans—our magic," Tor says.

His voice is raised in frustration, pulling a growl from Colt as he makes a subtle shift towards Mira. Not for the first time, I wonder if there is more to their relationship than that of bickering friends. When we all were young, Mira and Colt were always sniping at each other but were rarely found apart. Most of us assumed that they would end up activating a mate bond once they came of age. But, to my knowledge, a bond never formed.

After rolling her eyes at Colt, Mira turns her attention back to Tor.

"You would think that they would see the importance, or how it could easily bleed into their land. But my aunt once ignored a rampaging boar that had injured several neighbors simply because it was two strides outside her designated territory."

Cal blinks. "Two strides?"

"She measured."

A beat of stunned silence. Then a low whistle from Colt.

"They are not bad. They keep to themselves. And, from what I gathered, they have their own issues that they are dealing with. Though it has been years since I have been in contact with my family. And they never really told me anything when I lived with them either."

Gemma sighs. "So, we should not hope for help."

"I will send a message to my cousin," Mira offers with a small shrug.

"What about the wolves?" I ask, knowing that Cal has arranged an alliance of sorts with the Nights.

"They would help if we ask. But..." Cal closes his eyes, taking a breath. "My sister, Juniper, is alive," he admits.

I feel my eyes bulge out in surprise. "I thought..."

"I did too," he says. "My grandmother had a vision before the attack and saved Juni. About two years ago, she was found by the Nightfury Alpha's Mate and they adopted her. Other than Willa and the rest of my cadre, nobody is to know that she survived. They will keep her safe, but I do not want to deliver rebels to their doorstep. She is Sun Kissed."

"Of course," I agree easily. It is a miracle that the child survived and is imperative that she remains protected. "Would the other Alpha's help?"

"We will not ask that of them unless there is no other option."

The door bangs open.

Willa enters first, pulling Freya in behind her. Both of the women have eyes that are bright with mischief and curiosity.

"So," Willa announces, hands on hips, "what are we planning? And why was I not invited? I'm excellent at planning."

My heart does a peculiar bend whenever Freya comes into view. She is not golden right now—her magic is quiet—but she glows anyway, in a way only I seem to notice. She sidles up to me, brushing her shoulder against my arm, and my pulse steadies just from her nearness.

"We were not excluding you," I say.

"Yes you were," Willa replies.

"We were only delaying your arrival," Tor corrects.

"I expect a little edging from Cal," Willa replies, "not from *all* of you."

Freya and Mira snicker.

"It was solely for the sake of order," Kiran explains.

"And for our sanity," Gemma mutters.

Freya gasps dramatically. "Rude! Accurate, but rude." She slides onto my lap, perching her perfect ass directly over my now hardening cock. "Why didn't you wake me, Chief?" Her voice is raspy as her lips brush my ear. "It is not like you to leave me alone and unsatisfied."

My bear growls, not liking that we left our Mate in such a way. "Believe it or not, Mo Sholas, I did try to wake you."

"Tomorrow," she says, grinding herself against my solid length, "try harder."

I take her mouth with mine, unable to restrain myself from her sweetness any longer.

"Ooh yes!" Willa agrees. "I would like a nice, hard, wake up call tomorrow too, Stud."

"Noted," Cal smirks.

"What did we miss?" Freya asks against my lips.

"Doom," Colt says. "Possible doom, at least."

"Panthers," Cal clarifies.

"Lack of panthers," Tor corrects.

"And Sol has still not responded," I add. "It is unlike him."

Freya frowns, worry flickering across her expression. She chews her lip—her nervous tell—and I want to promise her that the world will not shatter, even if I am no longer certain. But before I can speak, the door slams back open.

Adan and Bo burst inside, breathless, sweating, urgency pouring off of them like heat.

"Smoke," Adan says. "North ridge. High enough to see from the patrol path. We could not get close without being detected."

Cal's body snaps upright. "Rebels? That would mean that they are moving away."

"Or someone else," Bo replies. "But it is not a campfire. Too large. Too black."

A quiet falls across the room. Like the mountain itself holds its breath. Cal turns to me and I already know what he is going to say. Because I feel the same pull, the same instinct. Go. See. Protect.

"We need to check it," he says.

I nod. "We will take scouts. Quiet. Fast."

Immediately, Freya and Willa begin to move.

"No," Cal starts.

"Yes," Willa says instantly.

"Absolutely," Freya echoes.

And then chaos erupts.

"You're staying," Cal insists.

"We're not," Freya argues. I bite my cheek to stop myself from smiling at her confidence to stand up to Cal. Of course, he would never harm her. But he is an intimidating being.

"It could be a trap," I add.

"All the more reason you need us there. We were sent here for a purpose. Maybe this is part of it. We can't just sit at home while you guys march off into an unknown situation. What would happen if you get captured? Hurt? Between Willa's blasts and my nightmare inducing illusions, we can help. Let us help."

I step closer to Freya, lowering my voice. "Mo Sholas. If something is out there—"

"Then you need me," she cuts in, chin lifting, eyes fierce. "You can Cal both. We're not letting you walk into danger alone."

My heart twists painfully. She is equal parts soft light and stubborn fire, and goddess help me, I love every facet. But the thought of losing her—of walking toward smoke and not returning with her beside me—sets a cold blade of fear behind my ribs.

I look over to Cal, where he is having the same back and forth with Willa. Adan stands near the door, looking like he would rather face a horde of rebels than witness one more second of this. Cal must sense that this is a losing battle because finally, he says, "Fine. But you stay behind us once we get there. Both of you. And if we say run—"

"Yeah, yeah," Willa waves her hand. "Run, hide, don't explode. We get it, Stud."

Freya squeezes my hand. "I'll be careful."

No part of me believes her. Every part of me will protect her anyway.

I take a breath, steadying myself with her warmth. "We leave in five minutes," I say to the room. "Light packs. Quiet approach. We will hopefully be back to the keep by dinner."

Everyone scatters into motion. Colt and Mira will be remaining at the keep to keep everything running. Kiran, Gemma, and Tor will be accompanying us to help protect our Mates if it truly is a rebel attack.

Freya lingers only a heartbeat longer, searching my face. "We'll be okay," she says softly.

I brush my thumb over her cheek, memorizing the warmth beneath her skin, the softness that the world will try to steal from her.

"We will," I promise.

And for her sake, for all of ours, I pray the promise holds.

# 27

## The Fire Bird & Her Shadow



Is it a surprise to anyone that Willa and I got our way?

No. Not one bit. And even though I truly believe that we need to do this, it doesn't stop the fear that I feel as I climb onto Caz's back. I quickly flip through pictures in my head, trying to land on something that will be obtainable for me to pull off if an illusion becomes necessary.

And because fire can be so damaging, we are not moving slowly. My very large, very furry Mate bolts through the forest at a speed that would absolutely void any horseback-riding liability waiver.

Wind whips through my hair. Leaves slap against my clothes. The forest is so lush it practically vibrates.

Chicago was *never* this green—or purple. It was basically three shades of concrete plus the color of atmospheric pollution at sunset. But now, I look up at the leaves above us, splashes of color that I could only dream of acting as our shade from the blazing sun, and I don't think I have ever seen anything more beautiful.

Chicago was loud, messy, alive in its own gritty way. But this place? This place is alive in a different light. It breathes with us. It moves with us. In many ways, it feels like it is a part of my marrow. Or I am a part of it. Two sides of the same coin but dependent on each other more now than ever.

Leading the group, Cal and Caz set a punishing pace, weaving through trees as if they have made this trek thousands of times before. I suppose it is possible that they have. Caz told me that he grew up spending a lot of time here with Cal and Sol. Their families tied together by their Sun Kissed blessings and centuries of friendship.

It makes me hopeful that when this is all over. When the prophecy is fulfilled and we somehow manage to broker peace between the warring clans, we will not be forced back into seclusion. I love Caz's castle in the mountains. But I love it down here too.

I glance over at Willa, holding in a chuckle when I see her sitting on Cal's back, feet tucked neatly around him, looking infuriatingly graceful for someone who used to trip over pretty much anything.

Behind us, Tor, Kiran, and Gemma thunder along, each a different shade of hulking bear.

It should be terrifying, but it isn't.

Because once I got over the shock of this world, I realized what I truly have here.

A family.

Sure, they sometimes turn into bears, but these are people who have accepted me for who I am. And that is something that my blood relatives were never able to do.

Unlike Willa, who died on impact back in Chicago, I made the choice to follow the light. I chose to leave my family behind with the hopes of finding something better. Of finding peace.

I don't know how I got lucky enough to have that wish actually come true.

Willa twists on Cal's back, catching my eye. "This still feels insane, right?" she whispers.

"Oh, absolutely," I whisper back, leaning low so I don't get smacked by a tree branch and die in the least majestic way possible. I look around at the towering trees, the shafts of sunlight sparkling like stained glass through the leaves. The moss covered ground that almost glows like emerald velvet. "I want to paint it."

Willa smiles at my confession. "You should. You are an amazing artist, Freya."

"I want to paint all of it," I continue. "The forest. The mountains. The sky. The weird, beautiful colors. And I want to paint Chicago too. The real Chicago. The city lights reflecting in puddles. The way the alley bricks looked at sunset. I have never really felt inspired like this before. Especially by thoughts of the city. But I want Caz to see it. I want them to know the world that we came from. And I don't want to forget."

Willa softens. "He'll love it."

Caz, beneath me, rumbles a deep sound that is probably agreement or love. Though, it could also be hunger. Hard to tell with bears.

But then—

A new smell threads into the air.

Sharp. Acrid. Heavy.

Smoke.

Caz slows. Cal stops. The other fan out behind us, forming a loose semicircle. I straighten, heart kicking. Because the air changes.

Not in a dangerous way.

Not in an oh-shit-run kind of way.

It feels like a hand brushing against my magic.

A tug. A whisper. A pull that curls deep in my chest and unfurls upward like a blooming flower.

Like my heart is attaching itself to another. Calling my name without sound. It is different from my connection with Caz. But it feels familiar.

My breath catches.

Willa's gaze snaps to mine. Her chest glowing faintly, her magic responding too.

"You feel it?" I whisper.

She nods. "Yeah. This isn't the rebels."

"No," I murmur. "This is something else. Something that wants *us*." I rub my chest. "Like it is desperate. In pain."

Calling.

Connecting.

Recognizing our magic the same way our magic recognizes each other. But instead of the light that I feel from Willa, this magic feels bitter. Angry. Dark.

A growl rips through the trees.

Loud. Deep. Not from our group.

Caz surges forward instinctively, but I slap my hand against his back.

"STOP!" I shout.

Every bear in our party freezes mid-snarl.

The growl comes again. Rougher. Desperate.

I slide from Caz's back, pushing him away when he tries to hold me back with his paw. "It's okay, Caz. I can't explain it, but I need to do this. Trust me," I plead, stepping further into the smoke.

The closer I get, the thicker it grows, curling around my ankles, swallowing the light. The heat rolls toward me, but it doesn't hurt.

The pull in my chest urges me forward, heart hammering as Willa joins me at my side.

Shapes flicker in the black, churning smoke. At first, it's just movement. Shadows. Heat.

But then... A body. Curled. Still.

And above it, a bear. Huge, with a scar sliced down his face. Guarding.

The growl he gives shakes the ground.

"We want to help," I call out, raising my voice but keeping it soft. "Please let us help."

The bear steps closer, causing another ripple of growls to erupt behind us. But something about his posture—his trembling legs, his frantic breath—tells me he isn't a threat.

He is protecting.

And he is afraid.

He steps forward enough that the smoke parts for me to get a better look. His golden fur flickers in the flames that burn behind him.

Caz and Cal shift instantly behind us, magic snapping in the air like silver lighting as they step forward to join us, Caz's arm banding around my middle protectively.

He inhales once and breathes a single word: "Sol."

Sol. Solomon Maw.

My heart flips.

The missing Sun Kissed Chief.

"Willa," I whisper. "Can you push the smoke back? And the flames?"

She nods, though her face is pale. "I...yeah. I can try."

Willa steps forward, planting her hands over her heart, and releases a pulse of force.

It sputters.

Then fails.

The flames dance mockingly.

"Try again, Willa. You can do this," I whisper, knowing that she has never tried to use her magic like this before.

She tries again. This time, the force expands, a shimmering wave that pushes the fire back and causes the smoke to twist away like it's been slapped.

"Good," I say. "Again."

The third pulse hits the air like a silent explosion—pushing the thickest smoke back, revealing—

Her.

Her skin glows like hot embers in a cooling fire, flickering flames wick out on her flesh. Her body is limp, naked. Covered in ash—but completely undamaged by the blaze that engulfed her small frame mere seconds ago.

But I would recognize her anywhere.

"Sloane."

Willa gasps as we both sprint forward, skirting around Sol and crashing to our knees at Sloane's side. Her body is still radiating heat, but we both reach for her anyway, uncaring if we get burned.

Because she is *here*. Our friend who we thought had died in Chicago. Our friend who is clearly the third Sun Kissed sister to help fulfill the prophecy is here and we just saw her body overrun by flames. How is this possible?

"I don't know," Willa replies quietly. Answering the question I didn't realize I had spoken out loud.

"It's her magic," I deep voice says from behind us. "She becomes swamped with fire, so bright and hot that it overwhelms her. Large wings form at her back and she flies through the air. But it always ends in a crash back down to the soil, covering her body in ash and draining her of energy."

"Like a phoenix?" I ask.

"How do we help her?" Caz adds, crouching down at my side and pulling me into his arms.

"I do not know," Sol replies sadly. "Her fire overwhelms her. It is uncontrollable. She will likely need to sleep for the rest of the day. Maybe tomorrow too after this last burn." He turns to the rest of our group. "Have any of you heard of anyone with such power?"

"Our Mates are from Sloane's world," Cal replies.

"She is our best friend," Willa adds. "Like a sister to us."

"And they were also blessed with powerful gifts," Caz says. "Not the same as this fire bird, but stronger than any Sun Kissed blessings I witnessed.

"Do the flames hurt her?" I ask Sol.

"No." Sol shakes his head. "They do not leave physical reminders on her skin. She does not usually remember them consuming her. They do not burn me, either. We are not sure if it is because she is subconsciously making it so or if it is because we are—"

"Heart Mates," I finish for him. "Just like I am with Caz and Willa is with Cal. The prophecy brought us here. It might have even allowed us to find each other back in our world."

"I think you are right, Mo Sholas," Caz says as he presses a kiss to my temple.

"We should get her back to the keep," Cal offers. "She will be more comfortable resting there."

"I cannot carry her in my bear form when she is like this," Sol replies. "That is why it has taken us much longer to arrive."

"I can hold her," I offer. "I know that you do not know me yet, and your bear is probably freaking the fuck out at the idea of someone else taking care of your Mate, but I promise she is safe with me. And if we run into any trouble, I can cast my magic without my hands. I will not need to put her down to keep her safe."

"Sloane has told me all about you, Freya. I trust her in your care," he replies, eyes softening as he sees renewed tears in mine.

After we work out some logistics, and I realize that I am much stronger than I used to be thanks to the bond with Caz, Sol places Sloane into my arms.

Her body is limp—too light, too hot, too still.

Caz lowers himself so I can climb onto his back one-handed, which would be extremely heroic if it weren't also extremely difficult. Balancing myself *and* holding an unconscious glowing, fire-woman is a circus act that I did not train for.

But somehow, I settle myself, legs wrapped around his broad sides, Sloane's heat pressed against my chest.

Caz rises beneath me, solid, steady, massive.

I exhale shakily into her hair. "Okay. Okay. We'll get you back. We'll figure this out. You just stay with me, Sloane. You don't get to check out early, okay? We just found you again."

Willa climbs onto Callum's back. "We're ready," she says softly.

We start to turn toward home, when someone snarls.

Violently.

Loudly.

Right behind us.

The bears react instantly. Caz freezes, muscles coiling under me. Cal pivots with a thunderous roar. Kiran, Tor, and Gemma fan out in a defensive arc.

I clutch Sloane tighter.

And from the brush leaps a panther.

A very large, very shiny, very unhappy panther with copper eyes and murder energy pointed directly at me.

Willa and I screech in synchronized terror.

"Why is there a panther!?" I yell.

"Why is it snarling at Freya?" Willa cries at the same time.

Caz growls so deep I feel it though his spine, rattling my chest with the kind of frenetic energy that tells me he is not in complete control of his bear right now.

Then Sol—who has been slow to move due to exhaustion—suddenly snaps into motion. He shifts back to his human form, ash-streaked and bare, and steps right between us and the panther like he's done this exact insane thing a million times.

He lifts his hand toward the beast. "Stop."

The panther paces, snorting angrily, eyes locked onto me and Sloane. My heart is pounding so hard, it is hard to focus on anything else.

"Sol?" I squeak. "Do you mind introducing us to your friend?"

Sol doesn't blink. "I do not know him."

Willa gasps. "Fantastic. Love that. Very calming information."

"But," Sol adds, voice steady, "he has followed us since Sloane appeared in this world."

My jaw drops. "Like a pet?"

"More like a shadow," Sol says. "Always present. Always protecting her. Even from me."

Willa points. "So…he's like her bodyguard?"

Sol nods once. "Yes. Something like that."

"Do we know why he's angry?" I ask.

"Confused," Sol corrects. "Concerned. He has never harmed her. Only protected. But he does not shift. I believe he is unable or does not know how."

The panther snarls again, stepping forward.

Caz rumbles beneath me like a living avalanche. Cal's bear roars defensively as Willa gathers her magic into her chest.

And I—holding Sloane tightly to my chest—make the spectacular decision to slide down off of Caz's back to meet this confused predator head on.

"Freya, no!" Willa hisses.

"Trust me," I beg, my voice betraying me as it cracks with fear.

Caz shifts back to his human form once I have safely landed on the firm ground. "Mo Sholas," he pleads.

"I will be okay, Chief. He needs to know he can trust me."

Passing Sloane over into his arms, he curses as I step away, moving myself so that I am within arm's reach of Sol.

He doesn't stop me from moving past him, but his entire body tenses like he's prepared to tackle the panther if he so much as sneezes wrong.

Lowering myself, I make myself as non-threatening as possible. I'm not sure it will make a difference, given the snarling group of bears behind me, but I figure it can't hurt.

My throat tightens as I raise my eyes to meet his copper orbs.

"I'm not going to hurt her," I say softly. "I love her. She's my family. My sister. I'm trying to get her somewhere safe because she isn't feeling well."

The panther's ears flick. His growl warps into something almost confused.

I angle my body so he can see Sloane more clearly. Her tanned skin still faintly glows, contrasting beautifully against Caz's dark features. Her limp hand. The way he cradles her knowing how precious she is to me.

"We're going back to the keep," I whisper. "Where she can rest. Where she can breathe. Where she can wake up and we can help her learn how to control her magic so that she isn't afraid anymore."

A small sound escapes him. Less snarl, more whine.

My chest hurts at the pain I can see in his eyes.

"And I know you've been protecting her," I continue, voice cracking. "Thank you. Thank you for being there when we weren't."

I glance behind me. At Caz, Willa, and our mismatched, soot-covered family. Then I look back at the panther.

"You can come with us," I tell him. "We want you there. She will want you there."

The panther goes still. Silent.

Watching me as I lift my hand slowly, painfully careful, and extend my palm.

"I promise," I whisper. "I'm not taking her from you. I'm trying to save her. Help her."

A beat.

Another.

And then, the panther pads forward and presses his cheek into my hand. A soft, trembling touch that makes my breath break.

Willa makes a sound halfway between a sob and a squeal. "Oh my god! Freya's freaking petting him," she whisper-yells.

The panther leans into my palm once more before stepping aside, positioning himself right beside Sol like he belongs there.

After carefully placing Sloane back into my arms, Caz shifts and lowers himself down to the ground, letting me climb onto his back once more.

As a group—bears, humans, and now, a panther—we turn toward home.

No one speaks.

No one needs to.

We are not leaving anyone behind.

Not anymore.

# 28

## Unwedded Bliss

### Casimir

By the time we return to the keep, the morning feels like a different lifetime.

Freya refused to let Sloane go until we were all safely inside Sol's wing of the keep—the one where he spent weeks at a time while our families all visited Cal's home. Gemma ran ahead, arriving before us to ready a room for them.

Seeing that she would be safe, Freya gently passed Sloane into Sol's waiting arms. We left them soon after, with Sol collapsed into exhausted sleep beside her in bed and the panther dozing with one ear twitching on the rug nearby.

I do not wholly understand him yet. But Freya's hand on his cheek altered something in the air between all of us.

Trust, perhaps.

Or maybe simply necessity.

Freya's shoulders sag with each step until she is moving on will alone. I lift her into my arms, tucking her head under my chin as I carry her into the sanctuary of our room, helping her undress, and settling her into a steaming bath.

The water glows in the candlelight, golden and soft, as if it wants to soothe her as much as I do.

Her sigh when she sinks beneath the surface is a balm to my frayed soul.

"Relax, Mo Sholas," I say, keeping my voice low. "I will be back with food shortly."

She nods without opening her eyes.

I leave only long enough to fetch bread, berries, and the roasted meat she likes more than she pretends. When I return, she is melted bonelessly into the water, golden hair afloat like a halo, steam curling around her like silk.

Her eyes flutter open at my footsteps.

"Hi, Chief," she whispers, voice warm and soft.

"Do you have room for me in there?" I ask, already stripping out of my clothing.

"Always," she says, smirking as she slides forward, allowing me space to slide in behind her. The water rises with my weight; heat envelops us both as our sore muscles begin to relax. I pull Freya tightly against my chest, massaging her neck and shoulders where she keeps most of her tension. She moans at the relief, sending a bolt of heat to every place inside me that lives for her.

I gather her soaked hair in my hands, letting the water slick between my fingers. Slowly, carefully, I run my nails along her scalp, rubbing the tenderness away. Her breath hitches, body relaxing into me fully, trust blooming through her muscles like warmth.

"Caz," she sighs, nearly melted. "If you keep that up I'm going to marry you again."

I chuckle. "Technically, we have not yet been married."

She spins around, her mouth opening and closing several times as she processes what I said.

"We should," I continue. "If that is something you want."

"Is it something you want?" she asks.

"Typically, a Heart Mate bonding ceremony replaces the need for a commitment ceremony in this world. But you did not really get that either. I am sorry, Mo Sholas. You deserve to have it all."

"But is it something that *you* want too?"

I kiss her in a slow, drugging kiss. "Freya," I breathe against her lips, "I have wanted you in every way a male can want anything."

Her tongue swipes out to wet her bruised lips, but I keep going. The words rising like a tide I can't fight.

"You were the first warmth I recognized after years of cold. The first color in a world that had turned gray. You walked into my life and everything—everything—shifted its axis to face you."

Her throat bobs with a swallow, and it pulls something fierce from my chest.

"I did not just fall for you, Mo Sholas," I continue softly. "I collided. I shattered. I rebuilt myself around the shape of you. You are stitched into every breath I take. Into every instinct I have."

The water ripples as she shifts closer, her knees brushing against mine beneath the surface.

I cup her face with both hands now, thumbs brushing her cheeks.

"Our bond was forged in desperation," I say, my voice low. "A rush. A necessity. A miracle born out of fear that I was losing you."

I lean my forehead against hers, breath mingling.

"But I want more. I want the part where I stand before our clan—before our families—and vow myself to you with the whole world watching. I want the part where I publicly claim what my heart already knows is mine."

Her breath shivers out of her.

I slide my hands down her spine, pulling her fully onto my lap.

"I want every binding that exists," I admit against her temple. "Every oath. Every ritual. Every way the world can mark me as yours. If there is a ceremony that ties our souls tighter than they already are, I want it." I brush my lips against her neck where my mark rests. "If there is a tradition that marks your skin further with my devotion, I want it. If there is a word stronger than *Mate*, than *beloved*, than *mine*—I want that too."

Her fingers tremble against my chest, tracing my heartbeat that I know matches the cadence of her own.

"You were not just a quick decision that I made, Freya. I *chose* you. And I will continue to choose you. Every moment. Every breath. Every lifetime."

She exhales shakily, her forehead pressing harder into mine, voice breaking in a whisper. "You could have just said yes."

I chuckle, nipping at her lips before dragging her into another kiss.

"You deserve the world. Say yes, Mo Sholas. Say that you want me as I want you."

"Yes," she nods, rising up onto her knees before positioning herself over my cock. "I want to marry you. But I want it to be in our home. Right where we bonded. This time, with all of our friends and family."

And the look in her eyes when she slides down my length, taking me inside of her?

I swear it feels like the first sunrise the world ever saw.

Our touches remain soft, but possessive. Searching. Feeling. Claiming.

After we both shatter, I lift Freya out of the water and carry her to bed, feeding her some dinner, before tucking her down beneath the furs.

"Caz... I was scared today."

The crack of her voice guts me.

She turns into me, resting her head on my chest as I trail my fingers down her arm.

"When I saw Sloane on fire—even before I knew it was her—" she shakes her head. "Do you think we will be able to help her?"

"I think that you are capable of anything. And we will all do whatever we can to help."

"Are they bonded? I didn't see a mark but there was so much ash."

"I believe so. Sol's scent has changed. It was why we did not recognize him until he came into view." I press my lips to her temple. "If they are unbonded, I doubt his bear would have allowed anyone—even you—hold her while she was so vulnerable."

"And the panther?" she asks.

"I do not know, sweetheart. I think that he is hurting too but I do not know why. We will ask Mira tomorrow. Maybe she will be able to figure him out."

"I think Sol is right that he *can't* shift. I know he was afraid that I was a threat to Sloane, but if he could have shifted to better communicate with us, I think he would have."

"I was scared today too," I admit, tucking her closer.

She blinks. "You were?"

"Of course I was." A soft laugh escapes me, raw at the edges. "I watched you stand in front of a panther who could have torn you apart in a heartbeat. I felt you walk away from the safety of my arms. I worried that your courage would cost me the world. Because you, Mo Sholas, are my world. My breath. My reason. I no longer know who I am without you and I have never felt more myself because of it."

"Caz." Her eyes find mine as tears well in her lashes. "I'm not going anywhere. Not without you."

Our lips meet. Slow. Soft. Lingering.

A promise more than a hunger.

A vow more than a kiss.

We fall asleep tangled together with her head on my chest, my hand at her waist, our legs woven as if they refuse to be parted even in our dreams.

I wake to shouting.

Loud. Panicked. Echoing through the keep like a crack of thunder.

Freya jerks upright, hair wild, eyes wide. "What—"

I'm already out of bed, pulling on pants and tossing her a tunic. We rush into the hall as Tor barrels past us, shouting for Kiran to follow. Gemma skids around the corner, the scent of panic sharp and sour in the air. We turn the last corner—and the world drops out from under my feet.

Colt stands in the middle of the corridor.

He is holding Mira.

Unconscious. Limp. Bloody.

"Help," he croaks out, voice breaking. "I—I cannot wake her."

# 29

## Worth the Wait

Freya

The shouting doesn't fade as we run—it multiplies.

It ricochets down the stone corridors, overlapping voices bouncing off the walls until I can't tell where one ends and another begins. Panic has a sound. I recognize it now.

We round the corner and my mind latches onto one thing and refuses to let go.

Blood.

So much blood.

Colt stands in the center of the corridor, shaking, with Mira cradled in his arms. She's limp, her head tipped back, dark hair tangled and heavy. The red stains everything. His sleeves. Her clothes. The floor beneath them.

I don't really see Mira at first.

I see color.

Deep crimson smeared across gray stone.

248

Rust-dark streaks drying on Colt's skin.

Bright, fresh red where it's still wet.

It looks wrong. Like a painting that used too much of one shade until it swallowed the rest of the canvas.

"Help," Colt pleads. "Please. I—I cannot wake her."

Everyone starts talking at once.

"Is she breathing?"

"Where are you hurt?"

"God, that's a lot of blood—"

"Move. Give him space."

Cal is suddenly there, calm cutting through the noise like a blade. "She is breathing," he says firmly, fingers already at Mira's throat. "Pulse is weak but steady."

Willa presses closer, her chest glowing faintly as she tries to assess without touching. "Mira?" she murmurs. "Can you hear me? Why isn't she healing herself?"

Colt's knees wobble.

"She did not wait for me," he says, voice shattered. "She promised she would wait."

Cal catches him before he drops, bracing both Colt and Mira with steady strength. "We will figure this out, Colt. Whatever happened. You are not alone."

My stomach twists.

The corridor tilts.

For a split second, it isn't stone under my feet—it's asphalt.

Gray pavement painted red.

Streetlights burning harsh white and yellow.

Metal twisted in shapes it was never meant to hold.

The memory comes back in colors, the way my mind always does. Willa's blood, staining the glass of the crushed windows. Stillness painted in violent scarlet. Sloane on fire. Orange and gold, screaming in agony.

It was just a split second, that memory, before my injuries ripped me from consciousness.

But I will never forget it.

I swallow hard, forcing the image away. This is not Chicago. This is not *that* night.

"Freya," Caz whispers directly into my ear, wrapping his arm around my middle, grounding me. I lean into his comfort without even thinking.

"Is that all hers?" Tor asks, voice tight. "Colt, are you hurt?"

"I—I don't know," Colt chokes. His body trembles violently now, sobs tearing out of him in sharp bursts. "I should have been there. She said she would wait."

"No," Willa says quickly, her voice soft but firm. She reaches out to turn his face towards her. "She's alive, Colt. Focus on that."

"What happened?" Caz asks from behind me.

Colt returns his gaze to the woman he holds in his arms. He opens his mouth to speak, but all that comes out is a strangled sob.

At that moment, Kiran comes running into the room, not stopping until he is standing in front of Colt. The blood spatters on his arm glint in the light as he reaches up to place his hand on Colt's shoulder. "It is done."

"What is done?" I ask, my voice barely more than a whisper.

"Kiran, what the fuck happened?" Caz adds.

"Cormac," Kiran replies, turning his attention away from Colt to speak to the group. "Mira went down to the dungeon to bring the prisoners their food."

"She didn't wait for me," Colt says again. "She promised me."

"The rebel leader attacked her. He—" Kiran looks at Mira's lifeless body in Colt's arms. "He forced a bond."

The sound of my gasp is overwhelmed but the growls and snarls that fill the space.

"He can do that?" Willa asks Cal.

"It is the worst offense someone could commit in this world," he explains. "A bond between non-fated Mates is dangerous, even if it is wanted. It is why commitment ceremonies are completed between non-Mates instead. Did she complete the bond?"

Colt shakes his head.

The mood in the room becomes impossibly more bleak.

"What does that mean?" Willa asks.

"Is that why she isn't healing?" I add, already suspecting the answer.

"Yes, Mo Sholas," Caz replies, holding me tighter to his body.

"Well, what can we do to fix it? There must be something that we can do, right?"

"There is noth—" Colt starts.

"You can bond with her," Caz replies. "A bond with you could save her."

"But we are not Heart Mates," Colt argues, shaking his head. "We would have felt the pull of our hearts by now."

"She has never shifted," Willa says quietly. "She told me that her animal is suppressed. Maybe your bond is too? Or maybe it is not a Heart Mate bond. Maybe it is whatever the panther equivalent is. But you have to try, Colt."

"I can't just make that choice for her," he says.

I look up at my Mate before stepping out of his arms and walking towards Colt. "Do you love her?"

"Yes."

"She loves you too," Willa tells him.

"I know that we do not know each other that well, yet. But please believe me when I tell you that she would want you to make this decision for her. Just as my Mate did for me."

Everyone from Caz's clan already knew this information, but I receive a few shocked gasps from Cal's clan.

"I was dying. Caz bonded with me to save my life and I never, *never*, was upset with him for making that difficult choice."

"But it isn't a bonding sun. How can I?"

Tor steps forward. "Mira's cottage sits on a ley line. It is a powerful point in the soil where The Mother's magic is stronger. Panthers—well, from what I have heard through stories—panthers bond at ley lines with their Core Mates."

Colt is moving before any of us have fully processed what Tor said. We follow him down the hall at a run, until we exit the keep and make the short journey to Mira's cottage in no time.

"What do I do?" Colt asks.

Caz steps closer. "You need to bite her, forcing all of the love and care into the bond as you can. Then, I will help her bite you."

Colt nods, taking a deep breath. "I am so sorry, love. You deserve so much better than this, but I will do everything I can to make it up to you. Please be okay." His words are whispered, though there is no mistaking the power behind them.

Lowering his mouth to her neck, he bites.

As slowly and gently as possible, Caz lifts Mira's head to Colt's throat.

"She will likely wake when she breaks through," he warns. Cal steps up to Colt's side, helping to support Mira's prone body so that she does not fall.

"Ready?" Caz asks.

Colt nods, baring his neck fully so that Mira is able to sink her teeth into his skin.

We all know as soon as the connection kicks in. Mira jolts, flailing her arms wide before bringing her hands to Colt's chest, clinging to him as she drags pulls of his blood into her mouth.

"That's enough, love," Colt says softly.

Growing up from the floor, winding around their legs, vines spread, tying them together as one. Once the vines retreat, copper swirls, like tattoos, are left behind on both of their bodies. Mira reaches out, touching the torn fabric on Colt's leg, causing the edges to instantly sew themselves back together.

"Remarkable," Caz says with awe.

"Earth Bound," Mira says, her voice dry and raspy. "But how can—"

"Are you okay?" Colt asks her, checking her over to make sure that she is completely healed. It feels wrong to witness such an intimate moment, but I can't make myself look away.

Mira reaches up to touch her neck. "You—"

"I am so sorry—"

She presses her finger to his mouth. "You saved me?"

"I love you," he tells her. "I always have. I should have told you before. I should have—"

Mira rises up onto her tiptoes, pressing her mouth to his in a tender kiss. "I love you too."

Colt's smile spreads across his face, moments before leaning back down and taking her lips in a searing kiss. When he pulls away, they are both breathless and I am feeling things that I am much too embarrassed to admit.

"You promised you would wait," Colt says, voice raspy with emotion.

"I've waited my whole life for you, handsome," Mira replies with a smirk.

"Are you sure you are okay?" Colt asks again.

Mira nods. "I promise. But I am going to awkwardly request that all of these people leave my home so that I can be alone with my Mate."

Colt's pleased growl is enough to snap all of us out of our staring.

"Shut the door on your way out," he tells us, not taking his eyes from Mira. "And drop some food off. We have a lot of time to make up for."

"Get it girl!" Willa shouts as I push her out of the door.

"Don't do anything I wouldn't do!" I add, laughing.

Once we are outside, Cal directs Tor and Kiran to reassign guards to the dungeon. He also directs other clan members to do various clean up tasks. But I can't focus on any of it. Because Caz is looking at me in that way that tells me he needs me. His purple eyes blazing with the same desire that has my heart beating faster.

Within seconds, Caz has me thrown over his shoulder as is bolting back to the doors of the keep. The sounds of Willa's laughter following us in the wind.

"So then," Willa says, spearing a piece of fruit with her fork like it personally wronged her, "he ordered milk with his steak."

I pause mid-bite.

Let the silence stretch.

Let it work.

It has been a full 24 hours since Colt and Mira's traumatic but beautiful bonding. After Caz took me back to bed, we spent the entire day in each other's arms, with the plan of cracking down today, really focusing our efforts on learning to control our magic and prepare for the inevitable battle that looms in our future.

But I don't want to think about that yet. Based on the conversation that Willa started this morning, I am getting the impression that she feels the same.

"Milk," I repeat slowly, tasting the word. "Like cow juice? He ordered cow juice at a three star Michelin restaurant?"

"Whole," she confirms. "He said it helped digestion."

Across the table, Cal's jaw tightens.

It's subtle in a blink-and-you-miss-it kind of way, but I catch the faint click of his teeth grinding together. His fingers curl around his mug, knuckles whitening like the ceramic is the only thing standing between him and violence.

Somehow, Willa keeps a straight face.

I take another bite of bread, casual. Innocent.

This isn't nostalgia.

This is survival.

Because if we stop moving. Stop joking, stop poking, stop *living*—my mind will slide right back to blood on stone and Colt's broken sobs. To Mira limp in his arms. To the heavy, aching echo of the bond snapping into place so heady it made us all into pure *need*.

And I am still feeling it.

The aftershock.

The burning desire that heats my core.

That strange emotional echo that lingers when two hearts slam together in desperation. My chest feels bruised from standing so close to it. From the memories, however limited, of my own bonding. It feels like I walked through a lightning storm, avoided a direct strike, but can still feel the hum of electricity deep in my marrow.

Willa shifts beside me, eyes bright. She feels it too.

So, we choose chaos.

"I once dated a guy who cried," I say conversationally, buttering my bread, "because his sourdough starter died."

Willa gasps. "Man-bun Miles."

"Yes," I say fondly. "A true artist. He wore scarves indoors."

Caz doesn't move.

He's too still. Spine straight. Shoulders squared. His gaze locks on the wood grain of the table like it's suddenly fascinating. His jaw flexes once, hard, a silent reminder that bears are predators even when they're pretending to be civilized.

His bear is close. So close, I can almost feel it pressing against the back of my skull, restless and possessive.

Perfect.

I am just a few comments away from getting every memory of past lovers fucked out of my brain. It is exactly the distraction I need.

"I liked Miles," I continue. "He made kombucha."

Willa wrinkles her nose. "You have terrible taste." She looks Caz directly in the eyes. "No offense."

"My tastes back in Chicago were mostly based on proximity and emotional unavailability," I counter. "Here, it is more fate and proximity to a supernatural being with a perfectly pierced penis."

Willa lights up, leaning back in her chair. "Oh! Remember the guy I dated who thought women shouldn't read fantasy novels because it sets unrealistic expectations in the bedroom?"

Cal's mug makes a very small, very stressed crack.

I bite my lip to keep from smiling.

Willa is definitely going to get tied up for this and I know she couldn't be more thrilled.

"Derek," I supply helpfully.

"Yes!" Willa snaps. "Derek. He once asked me why I needed hobbies."

"Well, sure. Why spend your free time reading when you could be on your knees sucking his—"

"This conversation," Cal says tightly, setting his mug down with exaggerated care, "is unnecessary."

"Trauma bonding can be very therapeutic," I explain sweetly.

The door opens before either of them can escalate further. Kiran steps in, eyes clear despite running on little sleep since Mira's attack. Gemma follows, arms crossed, mouth twitching like she's holding back a smile.

"She is awake," Kiran says.

My heart leaps.

"Sloane?" Willa breathes.

Gemma nods. "Weak, but eating and awake."

I am already standing, rushing towards the door as Willa rushes to catch up with me. We don't knock—the door swinging open harshly in our excitement.

And there she is.

Sloane sits in bed, wrapped in blankets, with color returned to her cheeks. She is thinner than we last saw her in Chicago. And she looks tiny next to Sol's large frame. But she is alive.

Sol busies himself with filling and placing a bowl into her hands, guiding the spoon gently when she trembles.

My chest tightens painfully.

I thought she burned alive.

I thought the world took her twice.

I can still see the fire. The orange flames licking black asphalt. The black smoke that swallowed everything in the forest. Her still body on the ground.

I climb into the bed without hesitation. I *need* to feel her in my arms. To hold her and know that she is real. She is okay.

Willa joins me from the other side, arms wrapping around Sloane like she might vanish again.

We cry together—messy, shaking, relieved.

We cry for Chicago. For the lives we gave up to be here together in this world.

We cry for the blood and the pain that we endured to get us to this point.

And we cry because finally, *finally*, this truly feels like home.

Sloane laughs through her tears. "I missed you."

Sol's hand reaches out protectively, anchoring her while we fall apart.

"I'm not going anywhere," she whispers.

I sniff. "Good. Because I'd haunt your ass."

She laughs again—real and warm.

And as Caz and Cal stand in the doorway, I think, maybe this is how we survive what's coming. By choosing love. By choosing laughter. By choosing each other.

Every chance we get.

# 30

## *It's Only Begun*

Casimir

The keep is quiet.

Not the brittle quiet that comes before an ambush or the tense pause of hunters listening for breath—but the deep, earned stillness that settles only after blood has dried and vows have been spoken and the world, briefly, has agreed to wait.

The fire crackles low in the hearth, embers shifting like tired stars.

Freya lies sprawled across me as though she has claimed the territory entirely. One leg draped over my hip. Her bare shoulder pressed to my chest. Her golden hair is still damp from the bath, curling at the nape of her neck, the scent of lavender and smoke clinging to her skin.

She hums absently, distracted, thoughtful, tracing the pads of her fingers over the ink etched into my ribs. Not idly. Freya never touches anything without intention.

I let my eyes close.

I let myself feel this.

Because peace is a rare thing for men like me. And rarer still when it feels undeserved.

"You are staring again," she murmurs.

"Admiring," I correct.

"Mmhmm." Her fingers pause, then resume their slow exploration. "And what, exactly, are you admiring?"

I tilt my head and press my mouth to her forehead, breathing her in. "You. Your strength. Your audacity. The way you occupy space as if the world owes it to you."

"Well," she says, smug and soft all at once, "maybe it does."

I laugh quietly, the sound vibrating through my chest where she rests. "I agree."

I kiss her again, slower this time, lingering. I want to memorize the weight of her. The warmth. The way she fits as though my body has been waiting its entire life to be claimed by hers.

She sighs—and then I feel it.

The shift.

The moment her thoughts turn sharp.

"Do you think it will be enough?" she asks.

The words are quiet, but they land heavy.

I don't answer right away. I know better. Freya doesn't ask questions she hasn't already considered from every angle. She isn't asking about *us*.

She's asking about what comes next.

She lifts her head slightly, her chin resting on my chest now, eyes searching my face. Gold flecked with green. Too perceptive for her own good.

"You, Mo Sholas," I say gently, "are more than enough. You are everything."

She huffs. "That is not what I asked."

"No," I admit. "But it is still true."

She studies me for a long moment, then exhales and lets her head fall back against me. Her fingers curl into my skin as if anchoring herself.

"I can't stop thinking about her," she says.

Sloane.

I feel the name like a spark beneath my ribs.

"Do you think she remembers?" Freya continues, her voice quieter now, threaded with fear she would never voice aloud to anyone else. "When it happens. When the fire takes her. Does she feel herself burning?"

My jaw tightens.

I could see the blaze as it engulfed her body in the forest. The fire was so hot, it would melt iron. I cannot imagine what it does to a body that feels everything.

"I wanted to ask," she says, her fingers pressing harder, "but I'm afraid of the answer. Because if she does—if she feels it—how can we ask her to keep doing this? How can we expect her to endure that kind of agony over and over again while the rest of us stand safely behind our magic and our claws?"

Her voice cracks, just slightly.

"How can I weave illusions," she whispers, "while she turns to ash?"

I stare up at the ceiling, at the beams scarred by centuries of war, and I feel something old and furious coil in my chest.

"I will talk to Sol," I say finally.

Freya stiffens—not much, but enough that I notice.

"He watches her," I continue carefully. "Closely. Not like a guard. Like a man who knows exactly how fragile a thing can be when it burns too bright. He feels her joy and her pain in his heart, just as I can feel yours. If she suffers the burn, he would feel it too."

"He is hard to read. Like there is a lot more going on than what he chooses to show the world."

"Yes," I say. "Just like Cal and I, Sol lost everything when the rebels attacked. But he was witness to their suffering. And his pain, if possible, runs deeper."

I think of Sol standing in the forest as the smoke cleared. Even knowing that it was Cal and I, he remained positioned so his back was never fully exposed. The way his hands tensed at his sides. The way his face now bears a constant reminder of the pain he endured.

The attack took his family.

But it took something else too.

"I think," I add slowly, "helping Sloane may be the only way he remembers how to breathe."

Freya tilts her head again, studying me. "And if it hurts her?"

"Then we find another way," I say without hesitation. "None of this—not the war, not the prophecy, not destiny itself—is worth her suffering."

She searches my face, as if testing the truth of it.

Then she nods, once. Sharp. Resolute.

"There's also the panther," she says.

Ah.

Yes.

The shadow that does not speak.

The one who never shifts.

"He hasn't left her side," Freya continues. "Not once. Even when she doesn't notice him, he's there. Watching. Guarding."

"He's not bonded," I say.

"But he's protecting her like it's a debt," she replies. "Or a promise."

I frown. "No one knows why."

"And that," Freya says lightly, though her eyes are sharp, "is what worries me."

The fire pops, a log shifting. Outside, the wind moves through the high stone corridors of the keep, carrying with it the scent of snow and iron and something...waiting.

"The prophecy is not done with us," Freya says.

"No," I agree. "It's only begun."

I think of the words scrawled across ancient scrolls. Words talking of a war that is on the horizon. Of stepping from the shadows and claiming our place in the light. Of a Sister's power to turn the tide and end plague on our land.

"We are all pieces," I murmur. "Not just us, but Cal and Willa. Sloane and Sol. Even the panther must have a role to play. We just don't know it yet."

Freya smiles faintly. "You make it sound so ominous."

"I mean it to be honest."

She shifts, pushing herself up just enough to kiss me—soft, sure, grounding.

"Whatever comes," she says against my mouth, "we face it together."

I cup her cheek, my thumb brushing her skin. "Always."

She settles back against me, her breathing evening out, exhaustion finally claiming her. Within minutes, she's asleep, trusting me to keep watch.

I stare into the fire long after.

Because peace never lasts.

Because fire must be tempered.

Because somewhere in the keep, a phoenix dreams of burning.

And somewhere in the dark, a man who has already lost everything will soon be asked to save the world—one trembling flame at a time.

And when that story begins—

Nothing will ever be the same.

# Author's Note

Phew. Another story down with only one more to go in this series. I have to reiterate what I said after completing Light Claw. Creating this series felt like breathing deeply alongside my characters. Watching them stumble, mourn, rage, and ultimately grow has been heartbreaking, funny, and unexpectedly healing for me. Through their journeys, they reminded me that grief takes many forms, and that friendship can carry you farther than you ever imagined.

In many ways, Freya is me on a page. Her sense of humor is exactly my own and many of her vulnerabilities are those that I have experienced during different phases of my life. All of our MMCs in this series are living through grief. But our FMCs are all experiencing it too, in different ways. Freya chose to leave her old life behind, but that isn't a decision that she makes lightly. And it doesn't erase the feelings that she has about missing her old life. Freya is a great reminder that joy and pain can happen at the same time.

I want to say thank you to all of my readers. Without the support that I received from my debut series, The Moon Touched Chronicles, I never would have had the confidence to continue sharing my work with the world.

Now buckle up book babes—because Ignite Maw is definitely going to bring the heat.

# Also By
# Ruby Ellis

## The Moon Touched Chronicles
Nightfang (Rowan & War)
Nighthowl (Ramsey & Griffin)
Nightfury (Reese & Bade)

## The Sun Kissed Scrolls
Light Claw (Willa & Callum)
Bright Paw (Freya & Casimir)
Ignite Maw (Sloane & Sol)


www.rubyellisauthor.com

www.tiktok.com/@author.ruby.ellis


Freya & Caz's book might be complete, but you don't need to say goodbye yet. Both characters, along with Willa & Cal, will make frequent appearances in Sloane & Sol's story.

Keep reading for an exclusive sneak peek of Ignite Maw, the final book in The Sun Kissed Scrolls trilogy.

# Sloane

"I have another one for you."

I can hear Jude snort through the phone, already amused by my pathetic life. Jude is a high school guidance counselor and he is always eager to hear about my dating disasters as soon as they happen. I think that being surrounded by teenagers all day has turned him into quite the gossip.

"What was it this time? A CPA who can't get it up or an ancient sleazeball looking for wife number three?"

I chuckle. "Neither. Well, maybe the first—though he seemed very confident in his ability to take my virginity and fill me with his offspring shortly after our spring wedding."

Jude's boisterous laughter rings in my ear.

"It's not funny," I scold, biting back my own smirk. "He called me Suzy."

"I'm sorry," Jude says, wheezing. "Where do my dear aunt and uncle even find these losers? This has to be, what, your 50th date gone wrong with people that they have found for you."

"At least that. Probably more. But you know, my eggs are drying up. I am running out of time to pass on our amazing family genes."

"You should come out and stay with us for a while. Give yourself a break."

Jude, my cousin and confidant, lives in LA with his twin sister, Josie, and her best friend Ayla. Unlike my upbringing, Jude's parents were the kind that a kid actually wants. Loving, accepting, don't consider their offspring as breeding stock. You know. Normal. Or, normal-ish, at least. Jude's mother, my mom's sister, is her complete opposite. At 17, she ran away from home, following her rockstar boyfriend around the world. It worked out well. She got a supportive partner, a life filled with joy, and two kids who she absolutely adores. Or, adored. Until cancer took her away from the world far too early. His dad followed behind her shortly after. They say that it was the years of living on the road that finally caught up with him, but we all know that he died of a broken heart.

When you have the kind of love that they had, it is impossible to live in a world without the other.

Soulmates.

Now, Jude, Josie, and Ayla live in a gorgeous but cramped apartment that is already busting at the seams. I could probably just stay in a hotel but...

"I can't right now," I tell him, not bothering to keep the sadness out of my voice. "Willa is really going through it now that her grandmother passed. She has been working herself ragged and hasn't been taking care of herself."

"Bring her with. Freya too. I'm sure you could all use a break. Besides, it is much hotter here. Maybe you will even find a nice billionaire to make into your sugar daddy."

I laugh. "That's the dream. I will think about it, okay? But I don't think Willa will agree to taking the time."

He sighs. "I get it. But the offer still stands. A break might be exactly what you all need."

"I promise I will think about it." Pulling up to the curb in front of a familiar building, my driver lets the car idle. "Hey, listen, I have to go. My driver just pulled up outside Freya's apartment. We are heading over to Lucky's to hang out with Willa until her shift is over."

"Ooh! You can try to pick up a husband there! What about Lucky himself?"

I chuckle. Jude has never met Declan "Lucky" Byrne, but he knows that the man is old enough to be my grandfather. Part of me thinks that he had something going on with Willa's grandmother before she broke her hip. He is nice, though. Fair, respectful. Maybe I *should* give him a whirl. If for no other reason than to see the look on my parents' faces when I bring Lucky to the not so surprise set-up dinners where they lure me in with my favorite meal and don't let me leave until I have been properly wooed by Chad, Dick, or Harry. Or, more accurately, Chad with the hairy and probably miniscule dick.

I make a mental note to run the idea past Lucky.

I say my goodbyes and hang up the phone with Jude right as Freya climbs into the car beside me.

"It is hotter than the devil's ballsack out there," she says in greeting.

I cackle. "What do you know about the devil's ballsack? Been reading monster smut again?"

"Again? I never stopped." She winks at me as the car pulls away from the curb. "I'm sure that every woman has a limit as to what is "too much" dick, but I haven't found mine yet."

I snort. "I'm pretty sure I found mine."

"That bad, huh?"

"I don't know why I continue to do this to myself. It used to be fun. I mean, I was never serious about any of the dates that my parents set me up on, but I could at least make a game out of it. Now, I'm just tired. Maybe my clock really is running out."

"Don't say that, babe. You are only 25. There is still plenty of time to find Mr. Right."

“Maybe.”

“Hey, cheer up. Do you want to know what I have done to piss my parents off lately?”

Despite still feeling a bit depressed, I nod.

“I exist.”

When I don’t react. She laughs.

“That’s it. I just exist and my parents are disappointed in me. Your parents are definitely going about all of this in the wrong way, but at least they want more of you in the world. My parents are praying that I don’t procreate. I am already far too much for their standards.”

I can’t help but laugh at her self-deprecation. “You are perfect just as you are.”

“Stop it. I didn’t say that to fish for compliments. I just want you to know that you are a catch. And I know that you go through with the revolving door of shitty dates to appease your parents, but if you ever decided to stop, I’m sure that they would get over it eventually.”

“I hope so. I just don’t know how many more dates from Hell I can suffer through without pulling all of my hair out.”

We pull up outside of Lucky’s and I make sure to school my face back into the boss bitch persona that I project in public. Willa doesn’t need my woes added to her own. And really, in the grand scheme of things, my life isn’t all that bad.  So what if I have to sit through a couple of hours of boring conversation aimed at my tits?

It isn't like this latest dude cared, at all, about who was beneath the Chanel.  He just wants a well-bred broodmare to fill his home and fulfill whatever family obligation his insipid parents forced on him.  We are different in every possible way imaginable but also, we are the same.  This life of clubs and pearls and corporate events is something that we were born into.  Maybe I should just give him another shot.

"Whatever you are thinking about right now, the answer is no," Freya says quietly as she joins me on the sidewalk.  "Nothing is worth it if it results in that miserable look on your face."

I sigh.  She is right.  "Maybe I just need to get laid."

"That's the spirit!"

As I walk into the pub, I let the feeling of comfort wash over me.  This is definitely not somewhere that I would typically frequent, which is exactly why it is perfect in every way.  The food is greasy and delicious.  The drinks are cold.  And while Lucky does stock some very fancy whiskey, there is not a drop of champagne in sight.

I know that I am fortunate to have been brought up in a wealthy family.  I am even more fortunate that I am able to provide for myself as an influencer—even if I am internally embarrassed that my entire purpose in life is to tell people what I like.  I cringe.  Maybe, one day, I will be able to find something that fills my cup as well as my pockets.

I joked with Jude about my eggs drying up, but that actually *is* a concern of mine.  Not yet.  I am only 25.  But I would love to have children one day.  I just hope that when that day comes, it is with someone who I love by my side.

Fire is not what I expect.

I always thought of flames as sharp, instant.  But this—this is everywhere at once.  It arrives like a decision my body makes without asking me.  One moment I am existing inside myself.  In a flash, I'm gone.

Heat blooms under my skin.  As if it is already a part of me and has just been lingering for its chance to break free. I wait for the pain to knock me out.  I wait for my brain to do a system reset.  To drag me into unconsciousness because surely, I am not meant to endure this agony.  But instead, my nerves light up.  Every single point of me is awake.  There is no edge to it.  There is no place to escape inside my own body.

I am burning.

This is the end.

I try to yell.  To shout.  To make the world turn and look.  To see.  To help.  But my mouth can't shape the words.

My lungs seize, instinctively pulling for air that feels thick and wrong and heavy. Breathing becomes a task that I fail immediately as I inhale smoke and ash. Each attempt chokes me, scratching down my throat as if I am swallowing something with claws.

My thoughts scatter. I try to grab one—move—but movement is no longer mine. My muscles lock, then jerk, then betray me entirely.

I am aware of myself in fragments.

My hands clench so hard, I can feel nails biting into skin.

My shoulders are drawn up as if I can fold myself smaller than the fire that engulfs me.

My spine is arched in a silent scream.

The pain does not spike.

It layers.

It stacks itself on top of itself, sensation upon sensation, until there is no baseline left. I don't know what zero feels like anymore. Everything is white-hot awareness, a screaming chorus of nerves all demanding to be heard at once.

My body is no longer a body.

I am no longer me.

Time stretches. Seconds become elastic, pulled thin and endless. I can't tell if I've been there for a breath or a lifetime. My mind keeps trying to catalog what's happening, like naming it will give me control.

*Heat. Pressure. Suffocation. Panic.*

None of those words touch the truth.

There is a moment—brief and terrifying—where the pain increases so much, it topples over into something else. A floating sensation. A distance. Like I am watching myself from a place just behind my eyes. I cling to that dissociation desperately. If I can step back far enough, maybe I won't have to feel it all.

But the fire follows.

It chases me inward. There is no safe space in my head. Every thought catches, ignites, and turns frantic. Memories flash without permission. The smell of rain on pavement. The weight of someone's hand in mine. The sound of my own name spoken gently. They all arrive unbidden and vanish just as fast, consumed by flame before I can hold onto them.

I am afraid. So fucking afraid that my heart hammers like it is trying to break free from my chest. Like if it runs hard enough, it can outrun the fire. Each beat feels enormous, echoing before it is swallowed whole by the roar in my ears. It stutters. Falters. Fails.

I think I hear screaming, but I am unsure if it is my own.

Beneath the agony, a strange clarity flickers. A knowing. I am being remade of flame. Trapped in this never-ending prison of heat and pain.

Still, my body fights.

Even as the fire consumes every thought, every breath, something in me refuses to let go. I cling to that spark. Not the fire, but the other one. The one that says *I am still here.*

I am burning, but I am not gone.

I am reborn in flame and fury.